EPIPHANY!

EPIPHANY!

A Collection of True Tragic Turned Candid Love Stories

JASEMIN SIBO

PARTRIDGE
A Penguin Random House Company

To order additional copies of this book, contact
Toll Free 800 101 2657 (Singapore)
Toll Free 1 800 81 7340 (Malaysia)
orders.singapore@partridgepublishing.com

www.partridgepublishing.com/singapore

CONTENTS

SYNOPSIS

This book is for all women out there who have been through a breakup, going through a breakup, or will be going through one but just don't know it yet.

ABOUT THE AUTHOR

** *It was a typical spring afternoon. An unsuspecting twenty-something year old grabbed hold of a pen and began feverishly scribbling down her past romantic liaisons and how in the end they became respectively..... botched.*

What started out as a therapeutic means to cast out nagging memories of her ex boyfriends' in the past had inadvertently made the author discover an uncanny knack in transforming each sob story into a candid, often times witty but most times wickedly honest chronicle.

These are the stories**

Note: No exes were hurt during the course of writing this book.

PURPOSE OF THIS BOOK

I have a simple mission with this inaugural book of mine.

To enlighten the hearts of my readers and make them go "What! And I cried a river over that guy?" when they reflect upon their botched relationships. It is my wish that this book will help my female readers find some form of closure in knowing that countless women have gone through their own frenzied breakups and stepped out unscarred and fully liberated.

I do not profess to be an expert in the much sought-after art of breakup survival. Nor do I proclaim to have a few glossy diplomas on psychology or human behavior tucked under my belt. What I do have is a recently discovered knack of transforming each sob story into a candid, witty and lessons you can take away chronicle.

This is certainly not a how-to manual or a breakup-survival kit. Rather, it is a collection of disastrous-turned-uplifting foiled relationship stories, beginning from my own personal experiences to various contributors' unique and colorful tales of the brokenhearted.

The journey starts off with my 10 years-worth of a somewhat sketchy but near-accurate recollection of past encounters with 7 categorically different types of men, and the invaluable learning after each of these episodes. These liaisons consisted of the First Love, the 1-Year Itch, the Office Affair, the Dark and Mysterious, the Super Torpedo, the Overtly Funny and Honey-I-Have Something-to-Tell-You guy, amongst many other illustrious characters from my plucky contributors.

It was certainly not a deliberate act on my part to have thrown myself into this myriad of relationships. I am still scratching my head as to how I stumbled into each one of them. Were they part of a divine plan aimed to enrich me with all these experiences in order to help others? Or was it just plain bad timing? I'd like to think it was closer to the first one.

HOW THIS BOOK CAME ABOUT

I first opened my eyes to this wondrous world twenty-odd years ago. As I wailed and cried my lungs out on that fateful day, I realized the passageway out from my mother's womb was not as taut as I would imagine. It was as if someone else had widened the passage especially for me, to ease my wriggling out. Oh joy, what a grand welcome for tiny little me. I would come to realize later on after proper formation of my brain cells that I have an older twin sister – Chloe.

Since the beginning of our lives, Chloe had always showed me the way to a lot of things. Like the time when we were two and she demonstrated the proper way of lapping up spilt milk on the floor, or the time when we were five and the older sister I looked up to deftly climbed up our living room couch which had been laboriously placed upright by us. I followed suit, fell, and ended up with a humongous bump on my forehead. Perhaps that might explain the bouts of memory lapse that I have occasionally.

Yes, I can never thank my sister enough for all her wise teachings. It was also her suggestion that I write a book based on all my ill-fated romances. Could she have seen an innate quality in me to reach out to others and give them hope of better things to come? Could it be her urging me to conquer my despair in a constructive and inspirational manner? Or perhaps she simply got too tired of the same "Sis, I have something to tell you" routine as I go on to amuse her yet again with another tragic account of a doomed relationship.

Whatever it was, I have decided to heed my ever-wiser sister's advice and thus now attempt to delight you with my tragic-turned-comical encounters with a certain species we women can't seem to do without; men. It is my wish that at the end of the book, those who have experienced the same heartache and desolation as I have will realize that they are not alone. That finding love is a life-long learning process and that everything happens for a reason. Yes, even with the forgettable Mr. I'm-too-sexy-for-my-love. And for events that just cannot be explained in any logical manner, there are always those voodoo dolls.

Just kidding.

PROLOGUE

You must be pondering on why someone in their right mind would decide to write a book based on accounts of ill-fated romances. What? A tell-all and spill-all book? Haven't you heard of diaries, missy?

I want to share with you what happened during my 29th birthday this year. Amidst pondering whether a chocolate or marble cheese would make a better birthday cake, I was suddenly besieged by a realization that this time next year would mark my 30 years of existence in this world.

This thought transported me back to the ripe age of ten, doing some serious contemplating on the whole meaning of life over a bowl of vanilla ice-cream.

I made a solemn promise to myself that when I reached the thirtieth milestone, I would make my first million and create an indelible impression in the business world. Yes, I would be the female equal of Donald Trump and my countrymen would quiver upon hearing my name. And yes, I would make such a great impact to society, that being able to scoff down my ice cream at one go would greatly pale in comparison. After all, thirty was like a few light years away at that time.

Splat. Back to the present.

It was pretty obvious I had to abandon my original childhood aspiration of becoming a tycoon, as no way was I able to catapult from my solid white-collar status to that of a billionaire business owner overnight. I decided to settle for second best i.e. to publish a book instead. There is still room for another J.K Rowling in this world, right?

Now back to this book of mine.

I have chosen to turn my many - nope, *manly* – misfortunes into something positive. I have decided to utilize all the teachings of motivation gurus (such as Anthony Robbins and Stephen Covey and the like), and will not and shall not succumb to the indignant dwellings of the romantically-challenged anymore. Where this is not a poignant rambling of a bitter and jaded woman, but a self-liberating journey of one woman, representing all those that have walked and tripped unceremoniously along the particular street called "Love".

I have tried reading books written by relationship experts, romance novelist, inspirational writers and almost everything that touches on matters of the heart, or rather matters of the heartbroken. As much as I give them my utmost respect and reverence, none seem to relate to what I have gone through, what my girlfriends and countless women who have had their hearts dejected have gone through.

Failed romances have become a common occurrence that plagues our everyday life. We have either been through one, or know someone that has been through one. But how do you graciously handle a separation and is there anything that we can learn from it? Can we successfully exorcise the pesky memories of our ex beaus from our minds?

Every foiled relationship is a very emotional journey and not to be trivialized. My book is not aimed to dictate what you should do to bounce back. But it is my wish that this collection of true stories from ordinary women like you and I will allow you to relate to what others have experienced. And through these candid tales you might be able to appreciate the lighter side of "ugly" breakups and perhaps find your way to self-recovery. No one is a victim of love; it was just not meant to be.

My dear readers, this book is from women and for women who have or will go through their own breakup in the past, present or future (but just don't know it yet)

It is a reminder to those that have experienced the same fate as most of us that life will go on. To bear in mind there is always some poor soul out there who has had it worst. And before you decide to embrace a lifelong vow of celibacy and adopt the term 'Boys' as your new 4-letter foul word, do remember that life has many more splendid things to offer.

For as long as we are still in the business of inhaling and exhaling, we will not lose hope. Women around the world, let us unite! There, not a hint of a skepticism or jadedness I dare say.

THE FIRST LOVE

It was during my first year in a university abroad, a bunch of us leaving our comfortable homes and having to live in a foreign country, where I experienced my first love. Perhaps it was the distance from my family, or the sudden emotional need to have someone by my side. Whatever it was, I was on cloud nine at that time. Or so I thought.

Benny was an easy-going simpleton, bordering a bum-scratching country bumpkin, some might say. He possessed exceptionally frizzy hair that threatened to break any hairbrush that came into contact with it, and would only shave his unruly bristles when they scraped my cheeks raw. People knew him as the bloke that tramped around campus in over-worn sandals and tee-shirts that have clearly seen better days. It is obvious now that he clearly mistook scruffy as suave in his attempt to project a cool yuppie persona.

Benny constantly walked around with a goofy smile and cracked the silliest of jokes. "Why did the zebra cross the road? 'Cause it was standing on a zebra crossing, get it?"

Apart from poorly constructed one-liners, cars were his other fetish. If cars had boobs, I would put my bet on him having a metallic 3.5 liter vehicle with low suspension and turbo as his girlfriend. Yup, that was Benny.

Our relationship was a typical 'Young hearts, run free…yadda yadda' bliss. Kym Mazelle could not have been more precise in expressing the feeling I had that time. And we giggled an awful lot.

Benny and I would mutually do sickly sweet things like delivering lunch boxes for each other at the university. You could hear us engaging in the occasional baby talk (yes, the guy as well) and even accompanying each other to the bathroom to wee-wee in the middle of the night – but only during thundering storms, mind you.

I really thought he was The One for me, that we would eventually walk down the aisle together hand-in-hand. And although we would undoubtedly have the usual marital spats with me complaining about his beer belly and how his rear end was having a more affectionate relationship with the couch than with me, we would still be considerably happy with little ones scurrying around the house.

I mean, he was my first love. I had no predecessors to compare him with. He bestowed me with my first sweaty-palmed hand-holding experience and my first sloppy kiss. At that point in time, everything he said or did was oh, so manly. And nothing-and I mean NOTHING –irritated me. *Dearie, I must say that was one of the most musical farts you orchestrated just now. What was that honey? You want me to give you a massage after I finish doing your laundry, clean your room AND buff your soccer ball? Of course my little honey buns.*

Frugal was also Benny's middle name. I fondly recall a black dress he bought for me for the year-end graduation party. I clung to it with a big stupid grin and happily ignored the $10 slashed down to $5 price tag that was hanging out from its hem. "He must have forgone his favorite hotdog this week to come up with the money" I thought. It didn't take a lot to impress my gullible innocence then.

Party night came and upon entering the hall I was, to my surprise, greeted by quiet hushes and discreet glances. "Gee, this dress must be a hit! The bumpkin does have some taste after all" I shamelessly assumed. The rest of the evening saw my dress gliding across the room accompanied by an even bigger stupid grin plastered on my face.

My moment of 'fame' was rudely cut short when my good friend literally dragged me to the Ladies and shrieked "Have you actually seen yourself in the mirror?" "What do you think? I only checked about 30 times" I wanted to retort. But never mind, I did it again just to pacify my friend who obviously had one too many pina coladas for that night.

The moment I turned around to look at the mirror, what greeted me was the reflection of a very visible lacy black bra and matching knickers: MY lacy black bra and matching knickers.

My jaw nearly hit the floor. Did some jealous girl rip off my dress when I wasn't looking? Did the dress self vaporize? And then it slowly dawned on me…. I had committed one of the deadliest fashion faux pas known to womankind.

The bright neon lights in the hall had inadvertently exposed my undergarments to the entire planet. The shoddy fabric used to make the dress was only slightly thicker than your usual Kleenex 1-ply tissue paper. My knickers never stood a chance.

This obscene silhouette then dashed out through the back door using hands as a body shield and jumped head-first into the first cab that she saw. "I'm going to kick Benny's cheap arse into oblivion!" were the last words echoing from the fleeting vehicle.

There is just something with our first loves that we can never replicate with the second ones and beyond. Maybe it was all the naivete and innocence that we still held close to our hearts. Or maybe it was an overdose of movies like 'Titanic' and 'Sleepless in Seattle' that unconsciously brainwashed us into hopeless romantics. Darn. Meg Ryan and Julia Roberts can be so convincing.

After approximately two years of being together, the first sign of impending doom reared its not-so-pretty head when we returned to our homeland. Benny began to drift away. Our daily phone calls trickled to weekly, fortnightly and eventually scarce need-be basis. He was not so eager to go out with me anymore. And even if we did, one of his buddies would tag along, at his insistence. Three is a crowd, Bozo.

I was dumbfounded. I did not know whether he had found someone new or whether there was something seriously wrong in the relationship that I was not aware of. Or in the worst-case scenario, had he developed a fatal disease and did not want me to know? I had even thought that it was due to his late realization that he was actually gay.

I mean, how could someone change so drastically in such a short period of time? There had to be some otherworldly answer for his 180 degree spin. I was plagued with hopelessness. What happened to all those lunch boxes and baby-talking days?

I persevered in my lone attempt to salvage our relationship. We had gone through a lot together, emotionally grew up together. I was gnashing my teeth at his sudden lackadaisical attitude. I pictured myself using a bazooka to blast some answers out of him.

I coaxed him to tell me what was going on, but it was to no avail. All I got were answers that hurt me more, and made me doubt whether I ever did know this person. *You go wee-wee by yourself now, you hear!*

After many attempts, I decided I was pursuing a lost cause. I did not want to accept it at that time but the old adage proved true again: the only constant in this world is change.

Benny had changed, and it wasn't his 3-day old underwear I was referring to. He was back in the comfort of his family and buddies and perhaps found no urgency in having someone by his side any longer. I sometimes think that maybe he did not change at all, but rather underwent a temporary Dr. Jekyll vs. Mr. Hyde sort of character shift when we were overseas, and reverted back to his old self upon our return.

After getting over my first failed relationship, I began to analyze, as I learned to do with the others to come, on what happened to us. I realized that only a few fortunate ones are able to make it with their first loves. I had girlfriends who had been together with their firsts for truly record-breaking lifetimes, like 2 years and beyond.

Vicky was one who had been going out with her high school sweetheart for 8 years. They studied together, shared similar hobbies and practically did everything together. Heck, they even started to look like one another and I was having problems telling them apart if not for their different hair lengths. That was how close they were. Then one day, out of the blue, they decided to break it off.

"Why?" we yelped. "Was there a third party involved? That bitch!"

But according to Vicky, there were no catastrophic reasons. They just fell out…naturally. No throwing of shoes, slamming of doors or even the expected screaming of various profanities, in multiple languages, mind you. Hmm, was there such a thing, I wondered? Jack and Jill went up the hill and both went tumbling over?

We reluctantly released her from our interrogation chambers, and slowly accepted the fact that yeah, maybe couples that stuck together like ultra-adhesive glues do fall out naturally. Of course, some fiasco would have made the separation more spectacular, but I guess this will do.

Reflection: So, to couples that have stuck together through thick and thin and weathered many storms and tidal waves, I just want to say one thing - lots of people envy you! Speaking for the majority of us that have unwittingly become part of the statistics in the failed first romance category, we really do wish you the best.

Sure, sometimes you may catch yourself thinking about rejoining the playing field, or checking out the occasional new male derriere. But how sure are you that the grass is truly greener on the other side? Was there ever a patch of green in the first place?

We weren't blessed with women's intuition for no reason, so I say, use it! Trust your gut feeling and that li'l voice inside your head. You will know it if he is meant for you. If your mind starts wandering around, just remember the curious cat that didn't quite have a happy ending in the end.

P.S: It is getting quite cramped over here so you lucky girls better just stick to your side of the fence.

THE 1-YEAR ITCH

Whilst I was rambling about my heart-wrenching relationship with Benny, I left out one itsy-bitsy detail. During our two year of supposed bliss, I developed a condition aptly called the '1-year itch' syndrome.

Note: Current medical reports do substantiate the fact that almost 1 in 4 women around the world suffer from this seemingly incurable disease, and medical practitioners are still zealously looking for a cure as we speak.

Okay okay, enough of the mumbo jumbo but during that time I had a fling with another guy. There, I can't be more blatantly honest than that. The bare naked truth in full glory.

I am still wondering how it all happened, whether I was under some magical spell or whether my wild streak got the better of me. Even though I could come up with 1001 excuses to get myself off the hook, I will choose not to. I have learned to admit my mistakes and this is one I shall humbly acknowledge. Till this day I cannot comprehend my motives for doing what I did. Maybe one day I will find out, maybe never.

Mental note: Another question to pose when I have my one-to-one chat with The Big Fellow above.

I had gone on a short holiday during one of my study breaks. Benny was never an avid traveler and decided to stay behind. By pure chance I bumped into Merrick the day I arrived at this new city, a childhood friend whom I have lost contact with for several years. My last memory of him was a braces-wearing scrawny kid cycling around town and catching frogs from the drain. Fast forward 10 years and he had blossomed into an impressive businessman, ditching the bicycle for a European sedan and his braces with a set of sparkling pearly whites.

I was elated to stumble upon a familiar face in the unknown metropolis I had journeyed to. He went on to be my unofficial tour guide, and we spent days reminiscing about our old neighborhood and engaging in heated debates over which one of us possessed the best frog-catching techniques.

Before I knew it, my holiday was over. "Oh well, that was a good blast from the past", I thought. Back to life, back to reality….

Unbeknownst to me, the minute I stepped onto the plane, I was consumed with this overwhelming urge to be with Merrick. I was flabbergasted.

Was I exceptionally frisky that week? Wasn't it just an innocent stroll down memory lane? I mean, we only spent like 5 days together. Could it be that the forces of nature went amok that day? Did our stars collide and started spawning new stars or something?

His image seemed somehow downloaded onto my mental database, and was invading my thoughts like an irreversible virus. Where was Norton when I needed him most?

I began to realize how different Merrick was from Benny. While Benny provided me with a sweet girlie kind of happiness, Merrick tuned into the womanly side of me. He made me feel sassy, sexy and desirable. He was composed and easily commanded attention in a roomful of people. He could speak fascinatingly about the most mundane things with burning passion: the make up of a classic debonair.

Merrick also prided himself as a culinary whiz and connoisseur of fine wine. He could whip up the meanest plate of spaghetti vongole in a jiffy. The aphrodisiacs in the clams must have been working overtime the particular night I gulped them down.

Tell me, how could any girl resist a guy that can cook AND is handy around the house? He even knew the cardinal rule of leaving the toilet seat down. And heck, he opened car doors for me! What was a susceptible woman like me supposed to do? Of course I naturally fell head over heels for him.

I plucked up enough courage to tell Benny that I might have developed some feelings for another guy, and that I needed some time off. I told him that I needed to know whether this emotion was real, or was it just an unfounded crush.

Surprisingly, Benny understood and agreed that perhaps a time-out would be good for both of us. During that time, there would be no strings attached and we were free to date other people. On one hand, I felt kind of relieved because we had sorted it out amicably. On the other hand, I had this sneaking suspicion that he had intended to do the same thing even if I had not mentioned it first. Things were solved pretty smoothly. Too smooth for my liking, in fact. Oh well, best to let sleeping dogs lie.

Benny and I had our time-out, and off I went to discover what in the world was happening to my hormones. My logic was that if I did later discover that Merrick was the guy I wanted to spend my life with, then it would merely have signaled a suppressed incompatibility I had with Benny. But if it was just a case of my hormones having gone haywire, my feelings for Merrick would eventually dissipate - and most probably I would end up with a big fat regret slapped on my face.

I have always been a risk-taker so it was a gamble I readily took. I just had to know and did not want to end up asking myself "What if?" all the time. Regrets or not, here I come.

Four ba-da-bing-ba-da-boom months later......

Boy oh boy, a girl's hormones can be real troublemakers. As you might have predicted, I learnt that my emotions had got the better of me. Yes, I can hear all the "I-told-you-so" now. Mind you it was not the usual wham-bam-thank-you-mam sort of scenario. But as convention dictates, those that covet while still attached will only find themselves utterly remorseful in the end. Not to mention utterly alone as well.

My inquisitive itch had finally been put to rest, whereas emotionally I was in pieces. Oh joy, my feelings for Merrick were not real after all. Oh boo hoo, wonder if Benny was willing to give us another try.

Benny agreed to give our relationship another go. I never really questioned him on whether he had embarked on similar self-exploration journeys with other girls. Ignorance was bliss, I gathered. As for how we ended up, my opening chapter is pretty much self-explanatory.

A majority of women will abhor me for saying this, but we are just as guilty and capable as men of 'straying' at one (or many, for some) point in our relationships. Yes girls, that is the nasty truth. And it doesn't just happen to your typical tarts, the outrageously flirtatious and the like. It could happen to anyone. Even plain old petticoat-wearing Mary. I am getting slightly alarmed at the number of married girlfriends I know who have ventured to Infidelity Street, and then back again walking innocently on their sacred marital paths.

Let me tell you little story about my friend, Rochelle.

Rochelle has always been well known, for lack of a better word, as a man-eater. And this bosom buddy of mine relishes on that fact. If you looked up Wikipedia for the description of 'promiscuous', you would probably find her name there.

Picture a red-headed woman, petite and fair skinned, having the mouth of a trucker and strutting around with a constant smirk on her face. Rochelle, Rochelle, and we thought tarantulas were dangerous creatures. Only God knows whom she had devoured that morning, or which guy she had sent home crying.

Rochelle never failed to delight me with countless anecdotes on her dates. Our lunch dates would usually start off with her grabbing my arms and licking her lips before whispering to me, "Do you want to know how my date went last night?" And before I could even order my Chai tea and biscotti she would begin to narrate the minutest details (length, diameter, girth) about her previous night's conquest.

This is also the same woman who has done 'it' in almost every public place. In the park, in the cinema, in the car, on top of a tree (alright, I was kidding with the last one). I once asked her whether she remembered the total number of her "triumphs". She replied in a matter-of-fact way "I stopped counting when I reached 30".

She maintains such open-mindedness in relationships (or what she defines as a relationship anyways) that she once announced point-blank to her parents "I think I am incapable of love". *Blink* *Blink*.

To say Rochelle is aloof is an understatement. But underneath the aloof exterior, there is a really strong-minded woman we are talking about here. Nothing shakes her.

Boss: Rochelle, you are fired. Please pack your stuff now.

Rochelle: Awww, really? I'll still get my bonus right?

Nurse: Rochelle, the doctor has diagnosed you with a very serious condition. You may need to sit down.

Rochelle: How serious is it really, Nurse? I have a facial appointment at 3:00pm.

So the first question we bombarded her with when she announced she was getting married was "Which poor innocent soul have you dragged into your lair for good?!" We found out later on that getting

Jasemin Sibo

a hubby-with-a-house-and-a-large-bank-savings-account did not seem like such a bad idea to her at that time.

Of all the infidelity stories I have heard, Rochelle's definitely takes the cake. Having been married for less than a year, over a tête-à-tête one day she tells me that she intends to get pregnant. Not with her husband, but with one of her better-looking ex's of different ethnicity. She reckoned her old flame had better genes you see. It was to be for the better of society, she selflessly claimed.

I could have just screamed at her. Darling, don't you think your hubby would notice the different skin tone of the baby? Duh! She probably would have managed to orchestrate this feat without a hitch if not for the aforesaid ex bailing out at the very last minute.

Reflection: Be it a one year or seven year itch it's still an itch by any other duration. Oscar Wilde's quote "I can resist anything except temptation'" taught me one thing – you will only be tempted if you allow yourself to be tempted.

What I think ol Oscar's point was simply this; why proclaim to your partner that you will be the most faithful girlfriend ever, when every week we seem to stumble into you, clad in a micro-mini at a singles-only party?.

If you can't keep a promise, don't make promises. If you can't remain loyal in a relationship, don't be in a relationship. It is really just as simple as that. You are just not ready, and it's not worth making everyone miserable, including yourself. Life only gets complicated when we insist in going against ourselves.

The cheating game has indeed gathered players from both genders in this new era. Perhaps this is one of the uncalculated consequences of the much-hyped gender equality in all aspects. Everything you can do, we can do better. And more discreetly perhaps? The folly of men at times...

Granted, I'm sure this is an art form most of us prefer not to master in. If you need a challenge, stick to mastering back-bends with limbs akimbo like yoga instead. Chances are it will be much more gratifying and you won't be eaten alive by your guilty conscience til day's end.

THE OFFICE AFFAIR

At this point in time, I was emotionally drained. Within two years I had experienced my first love, dabbled in a certain (ahem) frowned-upon act, got back with my first boyfriend and ultimately ended up with no one. I couldn't say I didn't see it coming.

Besieged by feelings of gloominess and desolation, it was then that Liam appeared in my life. The timing could not have been better. He was my new colleague at work, and had spent a good 10-plus years overseas. Liam was unlike previous guys that I have canoodled with. He was well-traveled and world savvy. Coming from a well-to-do family, he was surprisingly humble and forthcoming.

Proficient in various languages and having a strong propensity for business were some of his flairs. After just 6 months in the company he was already gliding across boardrooms and exchanging high fives with the head honcho and upper echelons. The icing on the cake was that he was excessively sweet too. Add this to his boyish looks and boyish charms and you'll get a concoction of endearing qualities. At first glance, anyway.

Not too long after we formed a friendship, he offered to drive me to and fro from work. The thought of not having to commute an hour a day proved too good to refuse. Soon, what started out as an innocent car pooling routine rapidly turned into something else.

Mental note: I would learn later on that I should have always heeded my mother's advice - never to board strangers' cars.

Going to work was never quite the same again after that. I would find chocolates or sweets left on my desk with small little love notes, and we would fully utilize the company's resources in sending out emails to each other every 5 minutes. The photocopy machine was not spared either. During lunch time, we would frenetically churn out photos of our recent outings at such speed, it nearly caused the machine to short-circuit and go up in flames many a times.

Lame excuses would also be created to justify late hours at the office. In actual fact we'd be having secret rendezvous around the office vicinity until the guards shooed us off.

At that time, he was Wabbit, and me Koala. Don't even think about asking me how we got those nicks.

During that period of intense er....car pooling, my ever well-informed colleagues started to warn me that Liam, in fact, had a fiancée. Of course I brushed them off at the first instance. If he did have a fiancée, I would have known, right? I mean, I may have been despondent and vulnerable but my eyesight was functioning quite alright, thank you. Even bats have other senses they could always rely on.

But I swear I could almost hear the beating of drums and clashing of cymbals the moment Liam gave me the nasty lowdown about his fiancée. I had to restrain myself from banging my head on the wall, or his for that matter.

The scene was befitting that of a typical Hindustani movie when the wife discovers her hubby had been keeping a mistress all this while. If only I was holding a pot of boiling curry at that moment....

Truth of the matter was that Liam's fiancée had lived overseas with him the entire period he was there. She stayed together with him, cooked, cleaned, clipped his toenails and toiled with various other domestic chores for him. The fiancée had not only devoted her best years to this guy, but dutifully followed him back to his home country thereafter. And to top it all, the fiancée was actually staying with him in the same house when that wretched Wabbit was out performing his daily car pooling activities with yours truly.

And I did not even have the slightest clue. Zero. Nada. Zilch. If not for bats, I would have been the blindest mammal on the face of the Earth. Just slap some wings on me, stick me with dark fur and I would have been ignorantly flapping away.

At this juncture you would imagine me giving him a piece of my mind before storming out from the room, puncturing his car tyres and stuffing the two biggest gherkins I could find up his exhaust pipe (I hear this can really damage the car). But no, not me. Somehow or rather he managed to convince me that she had become very difficult and that their love didn't exist anymore. Liam had every intention to break off the engagement even before I came along, and that he truly loved me, yadda yadda yadda.

In a batty way yet again, I flapped along.

I am sure most readers remember Glenn Close from her commendable performance in 'Fatal Attraction'. She portrayed herself as a delusional stalker who made her secret lover's life a living hell. Well, turn that intensity down 10 notches and that was how the fiancée was stalking me. I would at times see her appearing at my office, outside my apartment and once I even heard she went to my hometown.

It scared me out of my wits. From the moment Liam came clean about his other half, I kept asking him the same question: Would he have made the decision to break off with her regardless of my involvement? As banal as it sounds, I did not want to be the primary reason for their separation. I wanted an assurance that I was not holding the hatchet, but him rather. And whether I was in the picture or not, Liam was going to break her heart.

It took a good one month for me to finally come to my senses, and for the bamboozled fog engulfing me to clear. In a way, Liam had been diverting my mind away from my previous heartaches. The Wabbit had been my ricochet. But my guilty conscience went from tugging to practically yanking at my heart strings, and I just had to call it quits. Hey, I did not have cold blood running through my veins after all. Hooray!

The ending on the other hand, could not have been more Tinseltown like. It was on Halloween night, at his place, that I talked to his fiancée for the first time. I regret, however, to report to the guys that there were no catfights, nor were we clad in singlet and tight shorts wrestling in the mud. In fact, we were very mature about it.

After I got over my initial shock that we could actually hold a civilized conversation, I was bowled over with the discovery that she was actually a nice person. Not demanding and Primadonna-like as what her wayward other had been telling me.

His fiancée essentially told me that Liam would choose me in the end, and that she would retreat peacefully. I, on the other hand, told her that I was the one wanting out, and that I was truly sorry for causing her such grief. *Please don't ask the ghouls to gobble me*

In girl-power unison, the both of us confronted Liam. We gave him an ultimatum. The fiancée or the newbie. Choose. Liam would then tell us in the most clichéd manner, that he wanted me but had to choose his fiancée out of obligatory reasons. I even vividly remember him describing the love he had for both of us in arithmetic terms. Fiancée: 49%, Newbie: 51%.

And we say guys are not articulate.

This time I did what I should have done a long time ago. I gave his door a good slamming as I walked out, but not before imprinting my right palm on Liam's weasel face. (Note: weasel, not wabbit)

I reckoned I came out with flying colors after my graduation from the School of Hard Knocks. It was a difficult and bumpy ride but I learned the following: -

Reflection: When a woman emerges fresh from a bungled relationship, she unknowingly emits a sound that is only audible to dodgy and obscure guys (D.O.Gs). They suddenly pop out from all corners, scrambling over fences and elbowing other D.O.Gs along the way.

Bee boo bee boo......come and get it boys.

Epiphany!

How else can we explain why it is that the instant we break up, we attract the most dubious, problematic and confused lot? Never mind the various baggages they come attached with, the guy could be an obvious staring-at-you-in-the-face cuckoo case and yet it won't fret us one bit.

Dear ladies, let us not succumb to our vulnerabilities during these testing times. There's a survivor in all of us – it's just a matter of whether we want to let her out and do the necessary damage control.

In the event that one has just broken off and is at one's most flimsy, one should remain strong and not board strangers' vehicles. Stick to regular crazy cab drivers instead. At least there would be lesser chance for hanky panky and consequential regret eventuating.

DARK AND MYSTERIOUS

Following the Liam aftermath, I was back leading a non-dramatic life. No stalkers or dubious car rides in the vicinity. I was back in Happyville: peaceful, quiet and serene. I could get used to this.

And then I met Hans.

How should I describe Hans? In the most ineloquent manner, he was a cross between a Ninja, the Pink Panther and Maggie Simpson. Ninja because of his obsession in wearing only dark attire, Pink Panther because he was always snooping around in spy-like fashion and Maggie Simpson because I would later discover to my astonishment that he was also a cry-baby.

Hans had this dark aura surrounding him. Mysterious and dangerous. His naturally dark skin tone and jet black hair also contributed to this ominous effect. Always clad in black, I would joke that if he stood in front of a dark wall he would have just blended in. Imagine this wall with 2 big eyes blinking incessantly.

Epiphany!

Hard-core martial arts, treacherous spiders and car-racing were some of his leisurely pursuits. His 'death-mobile' stuck out like a sore thumb being the only one with pictures of skeletons plastered all over its body.

Extremely proud he was of his talents in smoking like a chimney and drinking like a goldfish. Being his leery self, he never left home without tucking a Swiss army penknife in his pocket 'for precautionary measures'. This I duly found out when I queried him about that pointy thing bulging under his pants.

Hans also mentioned to me various times that his life-long ambition was to become an assassin. How interesting. Till now I can't fathom why my girlfriends warned me to stay away from that 'cagey maniac'. Why judge him based on his slightly twisted aspiration? That would be unfair now wouldn't it?

True, his shifty character raised my eyebrows at first. But my trigger was tripped when he started leaving romantic poems on my car and secretly placing bouquets of roses at my doorstep almost on a daily basis. I was bowled over by his dogged persistence and decided that the dark side may not be so spooky after all. It wouldn't hurt to take a quick peek, would it?

For reasons unexplainable by science, women are prone to be attracted to men who emit a sense of obscurity. Hmm, his hand is reaching out towards the dinner table. Now is he going for that slab of medium rare steak, or the tomato and cucumber salad? Sigh, he is so unpredictable.

But his mystifying and enigmatic persona soon turned into an over-emotional 'I will die if you leave me' demeanor.

Our usual dialogue thereafter would sound something like this:-

Hans   : *You don't care about me anymore. All I do is sit at home and wait for your call but you never do. You are so heartless. What happened to you?*

Me   : *Dear, I am drowning with work. My idiotic boss is breathing down my neck and I have tons of deadlines to meet. Please understand.*

Hans   : *You used to make time for me. All you do now is work, sit in front of the idiot box or hang out with your buddies. What about me?*

Me   : *Come on, you know that is not true. You are my number one. Trust me; would I ever lie to you? I will make it up to you okay?*

Hans   : *Huh, you think you can just use teddy bears and chocolates to buy me over? You think I'm like every other guy don't you? Well I'm not! *Pout**

Me   : *If we are both so unhappy, why don't we just call it quits? No point dragging this any further.*

Hans   : *What? Are you trying to break up with me? After all that I have done for you? If you leave me I will just die okay. Please, let us work things out. *Sob* *Sob**

Whoa.......wait a minute, who was this UFO (Unidentified Feeble Object) that I was suddenly going out with? Assassins don't brood, and they definitely do not whine. Who are you and what have you done with Hans? I don't recall ordering a plate of wobbly Jell-O as my boyfriend.

That would be the last I saw of Hans the Mysterious, as Hans the Feeble would take reign from then on.

The next few weeks were like being concurrently trapped in scenes from 'Nightmare on Elm Street' and 'Urban Legend'. I had had my fair share of Hans's erratic behavior and I wanted to get out, pronto. I was scared. I told him we would not work out. And that we would be happier and much saner on our own. He did not agree with me.

When I went out with friends, I would sense this dark evasive shadow behind some trees watching me, only to find that shadow vanished the minute I turned around. Not before I heard the awfully familiar sound of his car tyres screeching away.

At my work place, I used to look out from my window and bask in the picturesque view of blooming peonies and cute little squirrels scampering around. On one occasion, Hans called me at work and in between sobs said something along the lines of how nice he thought I appeared in my favorite beige dress. I had no idea how he had accurately guessed what apparel I had on that particular day.

As I turned towards the window and wondered how on Earth I was going to get myself out from this sticky situation, there he was staring straight into my eyes with one hand tightly clenched against the window pane. I think I suffered a mini cardiac arrest at that moment.

Subsequently, he would undertake to call me in the middle of the night sounding very morbid. There was even once when he called and I could indistinctly hear sounds of something being sharpened. "Hans, what was that"? "Nothing, I am just sharpening my samurai knife". Okay. *Gulp*

I attempted to inflict reality into our now defunct relationship by going out with other suitors. Whenever Hans found out I was having dinner with another male other than my brother, he would text and call my phone every five minutes to keep tabs on what we were doing. "Are you at our favorite restaurant? Are both his hands on the table? You are not wearing anything revealing are you?"

Mystery had transformed into downright scary. I would attempt many times to break off completely with him but it got harder and harder as he turned more vulnerable and morose. Also, I was afraid he might do something to hurt himself, or me, or even his pet cat Fluffy.

But the last straw came one fateful night after what I thought was a friendly post-breakup dinner. He was driving and I quietly mentioned to him how glad I was that he had finally come to his senses. All of a sudden I could see the veins on his forehead popping out and he began to drive like a speed demon, the car swaying sideways Daytona style. I felt my grilled snapper making its way up my throat.

I lost my marbles there and then. I shrieked at Hans telling him to calm down, which eventually he did. Otherwise you would be reading a book with another title - The night my grilled snapper made me choke. Pheew.

After that close encounter, the shady one mysteriously disappeared from my life. A few months after that I overheard two women giggling about coming across this particular elusive guy who had been leaving poems and sending flowers to one of them. His trademark was the skeletons on his car. I caught myself cringing with goose pimples spreading like wild fire all over my body. I knew that modus operandi far too well.

I was on the verge of blurting out "What, he is still on the loose?!", but managed to refrain myself from hurling those words at the women to tell them about my freakish experience with Hans. I hoped for their sake that he had changed for the better, or at least got rid of his weapons.

I am sorry to say this but women can be such darn hypocrites at times. You hear us wishing to meet someone who for once is not the typical Jack-working-in-a-bank-and-likes-cars kind of guy. And when we actually do meet someone with a hint of hocus-pocus, we get all scared and start biting our French manicured fingernails. There is just no pleasing us really.

Reflection: Jimmy next door is sweet, tells you everything about himself on the first date and has never uttered a single foul word. On the other end of the stick we have Marcus, Jimmy's older brother. He's rebellious, chain smokes, broods, and has posters of Darth Vader and Evil Knievel plastered across his room.

How much do you want to bet that we'd probably have a secret crush on Marcus?

We lament about all the good guys being extinct, or guys being inadequate in verbalizing their emotions. And yet when we do come across these endangered species we make a mad dash towards the nearest exit. "Why is he telling me stories about his childhood? Is that a tear I see forming in his eye? Someone please stuff a pacifier into this cry baby's wailing mouth!"

I just can't explain it. A greater bulk of us gravitates towards the aloof and the standoffish. We may say Jimmy is the perfect husband material, but let's face it; it's really Marcus that we're attracted to.

We always want what we shouldn't get. You know it, and I know it. Maybe it's that thrill in dabbling with the forbidden, the can't-bring-home-to-meet-mom type....or maybe Marcus brings out the wild child inside each of us that has always been yearning to come out.

But the ending is usually a no-brainer —tear-soaked pillows and wishing we'd gone out with good ol' Jimmy instead.

My advice is when one gets attracted to elusive squid like men, avoid at all costs or else risk getting choked on grilled snapper. Normalcy may lack some luster but at least you'll have your sanity intact and won't have to contemplate enrolling under the witness protection program.

THE SUPER TORPEDO

One enchanted evening, Brad came sashaying towards me following a seminar I attended. I honestly thought he was a semi-celebrity what with his Eurasian looks and ridiculously soft hair. I cannot really put my finger as to who eyed who first, but the first thing that came to my mind was "Ooh la la".

His face could have been used in one of those underpants ads in GQ magazine. If you could imagine a Leonardo DiCaprio look alike donned in some cute little devil boxers, lying on a futon and making smooches to the camera, you would get my drift.

Yes, he was that enthralling ladies. *Growl*

"Any second now the paparazzi will jump out from under the tables and blind us all with their camera flashes," I thought with anticipation.

In what seemed like a sudden twist to the event, this ethereal being then started walking towards my direction. I began to mentally formulate a quick explanation about how I'm not with the press whilst secretly stuffing my phone number in his bag. But lo and behold, he asked for my number first. I flipped my head around to make sure he wasn't talking to someone else.

With my eyes shamelessly transfixed on him, I was mesmerized by his archetypal hypnotic allure that was oozing with charisma and confidence. Chocolate laced words and old-fashioned chivalry were his chosen weapons of mass seduction. Later, I found myself nodding fervently to his request of having a cuppa later.

Of course, you would be absurdly wrong to think most women including mua would have positively gone gaga over some pretty boy like Brad. I for one beg to differ. For the record, I did check for that thingy located between the ears first. Turned out Brad was intelligent and had business acumen. Oh joy, the old girl managed to bag herself a near extinct creature. Lucky me.

Gung-ho, vigorous and give anything and everything a go was some of the traits I would pin on Brad. Tomorrow or wait a second were words unrecognizable in his vocabulary. Everything had to be fast, fast, fast. And I mean everything. He even talked faster than normal people. Every time after hearing him speak, I would be panting and catching my breath, without me even uttering a single word. I should have plastered a big hazard sign on his chest saying: Those with heart conditions and high blood pressure should refrain from talking to this person. Converse at your own risk.

It would also be an understatement if I said Brad was adventurous. He could have been dubbed as the Christopher Columbus of the entrepreneurial world. Pinky and the Brain were his role models. "One day I shall rule the world!" he would always say, before trailing off with a sinister laughter. "Muahahaha"

Where do I even begin to narrate his many interesting endeavors? When I met him, he worked as a part time insurance agent and was in the midst of bringing in some top secret diamond franchise from overseas. Few weeks after that, he was selling some miracle slimming products.

That particular foray in the weight loss business would have probably made him his first million if not for some "complications" associated with the goods later on. I went hysterical once reading the adverse reports and was screeching at him for convincing me that they were okay. He just went, "Oh really? Has it caused a nationwide medical scare? Okay, guess I have to discard them then. Next!"

Hello! What have you made me ingest you dope.

Brad frequently claimed he could sell sand to the Arabs, and ice to the Eskimos. He even aptly proclaimed himself to be "The Emperor", the great almighty one. With his suave and silver tongue, I never doubted that. I counted my blessings for not being one that resided in an igloo.

Throughout the course of our relationship, Brad would be pottering around in his various attempts in making him a billionaire. He dabbled in selling cutlery, selling guns (paintball guns that is) selling land, selling cigars, selling airplanes, selling furniture, selling wine etc. If it could bring in the moolah, he would sell it. Heck, if I could made money for him, he would have traded me in too. Bids for a hale and hearty old cow anyone? Going once, twice, twice and a half…. anyone?

But I learnt nothing is ever idyllic. Everything is perfectly flawed, one way or another. As much as I admired Brad's drive, he sucked at being in a relationship. Let us just say he was practically hopeless.

He once gave me a short briefing on what the term girlfriend meant to him. In his very own words: -

#1 A girlfriend was someone that slogged around the clock to answer his every beck and call (short of kowtowing to him and kissing the ground that he walked on).

#2 A girlfriend was also a master chameleon that acted as a masseur whenever his joints ached just a wee bit, but in a snap of a finger must quickly assumed the position of his umbrella girl at his motor cross races (amongst other extreme sports he would have a crack at).

#3 If he developed a sudden craving for fried chicken in the dead of the night, you better be ready to scour the city in search of it in no more than 10 minutes time. Resourcefulness and speedy responses were a must, while making him wait was a big no-no.

Brad also believed that in a relationship there should be no expectations set, and that we should leave things to the forces of nature, the yin and the yang, the karma and the sutra.

"Huh? You want me to come over because you are having epilepsy? Now, now, I sense some expectations there sweetie."

And what was the most romantic gesture the dynamite did for me? Upon returning from one of his many business trips, he shoved me this crinkly, sticky plastic bag bundle, which I seriously thought contained some poor demised creature called Bob. It was in fact a cute little teddy bear all trapped inside this hideous exterior.

Who said romance was dead?

Brad didn't need a girlfriend, he needed a companion. I would explain to him the whole concept of a girlfriend, only with him saying "Girlfriend, masseuse, companion, and domestic helper, what's the difference?" Dim wit.

Despite all this, I persevered to change his perceptions and for the next few months saw me knocking, drilling and close to jack-hammering the correct ideology into his thick head. After a few successive soft badgering sessions, he finally came clean.

Brad wasn't at all interested in life-long commitments, holy matrimony or any of that stuff. Having a girlfriend or a wife for that matter never really crossed his mind. What he was really after, was just a pair of healthy fertile ovaries simply for procreation purposes.

You see, he had been harboring this life-long ambition of raising a child all on his own (just like in his case). Unfortunately, a wife was never in the picture. His convertible just had enough space to fit him and the bub I'm afraid.

At that instant it all came crashing down on me. His constant compliments on my curvaceous and well endowed behind were actually his real thoughts of "Hmm, your sizable arse and wide hips should be able to bear me with plenty healthy offspring. My legacy will definitely live on."

"I turned out pretty alright didn't I?" he proceeded. Well, if you turned a blind eye to his narcissistic nature and tossed aside his skewed perception of women as purely child-producing machines, I suppose he could have turned out far worst.

I caught myself turning misty eyed, not because I was touched by his noble intention of being a single parent, but out of pure commiseration for his future unsuspecting bearer of all the Brad juniors.

I had been in love with the idea of Brad, whereas Brad himself left much to be desired.

Music: You're just too good to be true...can't take my eyes off of you...you feel like heaven to touch.....if only you were not such a muck.

It may have been his overpowering focus on one thing – himself. Or it could have been his much skewed perception of what constituted a girlfriend. Although he meant no harm, obviously we were on different tracks. Hence I disembarked from the ever changing tableau of Dynamo Express.

Why oh why are women so spellbound by men that seemed to be in command and competent? Take the case of my dear old brother. Okay, he may not possess the looks of Tom Cruise or David Beckham, his belly can substitute that of a trampoline, and his crowning glory is fast turning into a case of tapering vicinity. But he is one bouncing leaping dynamo. Similar to Brad, he is very career driven, a go-getter and very sure of himself.

Two women literally fought over him, my trampoline brother. These were not your typical catty tarts I am talking about. They were so tame and demure they could have passed as nuns. But I guess hell knows no wrath like a woman challenged.

They recounted the days when they would race each other to meet him after work. The rule was that whoever arrived first would get to go out with him. When they went on a group trip, you would find these two ladies co-operatively slathering my brother with sun tan lotion. One slightly above the mid rift and the other slightly below. The mid rift was the sacred temple you see. It was zoned off.

This three-way relationship dragged on for about two years before my dear brother finally made his decision. The 'winner' is now my beloved sister-in-law, and just recently over some burnt pancakes and bananas we reminisced about the so called battle that she had won. She threw down her fork and huffed "I must have been possessed then because I still can't fathom how I endured all those heartaches and shameless acts. Sure, your brother was charming and ambitious but at times I take pleasure fantasizing about shaving off whatever hair he has left!"

They are still a happy bickering couple, but my sis-in-law still can't help but to advise me time and time again never to follow her footsteps. "Them dynamos....you can never catch up with them. And when you do, you have to hang on with your dear life or else you'll get flung into the deep ravine." That might explain the crash helmet that she carries with her everywhere.

Despite all this and with you as my witness, let me be one to vouch that so long as there are capable men left out there, there will be continued acts of shame and fighting for mid rifts from us women.

Don't you just love us?

Reflection: It dawned on me that women in general may be clutching this instinctive need to find men that took charge. We maintain this secret desire for someone strong and noble to pave the way while we act as the eager followers.

Could it all have begun during the stone-age era? Where men would go about doing their hunting business and when returning would lug the women by their hair into their caves for some procreation action?

Nah.

Certainly that's all a blast in the past now. Smack me hard and call me Daisy if there's something that a woman can't do now. We've walked on the moon, ruling presidents of a few countries, and won't even flinch behind the wheels of a monster truck.

There's no denying that most of us will still find the dynamic and suave captivating, and there's absolutely nothing wrong with that. But just make sure he's not under the impression that the solar system revolves around him, and he has passed a basic course in Girlfriend 101.

THE OVERTLY FUNNY

Those that do not find witty men sexy please raise their hands. Just as I thought. Hands down zilch. If the way to a man's heart is through his stomach, then the way to a woman's is through her funny bone. Just tickle it like crazy. We all want men to.

Your first impression of Olivier may be something like: spiky hair, pretty normal looks, bespectacled, fairly small built for a guy, sporadic snobbish outbursts, blatantly honest and definitely ain't that tall at all.

However, as the world is fair in its own mystic ways, Olivier was blessed with the ability in making even staid Aunt Maida snickering with glee. A wise one once said, what you lack in one department will always be compensated in another. Olivier's was his height (or lack thereof) but his comedic appeal could put Bozo the Clown to complete shame.

Guys, allow me to let you in on a little secret. Dashing looks or winning smiles are not must-haves to make us swoon. You may even look like you were dropped on your face when you were a baby, but given you religiously follow and attempt to mimic punch lines from quality shows such as Dumb & Dumber and the like; you are on your way mister.

I can't recollect which particular one-liners Olivier pulled that got me, but for your reading pleasure, some of the more memorable ones were:

If salsa is hot and spicy, can you be my salsa and me your taco so that I can dip inside you?

Do you like puppies? Cause there is a little pup inside my pants that needs some petting.

Pretty girl, why don't I give you a quarter and you can call your dad and tell him you ain't coming home tonight.

You can stop praying now cause I am the answer to your prayers.

Did I get you at hello? No? I'll walk out the door and try again.

Uncle Tom says you used to run around naked as a child. Can you re-enact that for me?

I see you are looking bored. Want to play doctor?

Hey darling, I reckon the dress you are wearing would look much better around your ankles.

And the all time favorite;

Epiphany!

Help! My friend Dick is having trouble breathing. Can you perform CPR on him?

With charming (not) quips like that, how could any female not go bonkers? If Austin Powers had a long lost brother, Olivier might have been it. Oh baby, behave. *Snarl*.

I tell you, we can be such suckers when it comes to guys with the slightest sense of humor. Yes, we can be that gullible. Look at Austin Powers. Need I say more?

Due to Olivier's nifty knack, he became all the girls' favorite. Where is Olivier? Why is he not here? What do you mean his favorite aunt is in a coma?

Initially I was delighted with my girlfriends' fondness for him. I made them proud as gone were my assassin and wabbit days. However, I had this sneaking suspicion that Funny Boy was having just a tad bit too much fun basking in all this attention. And something smelled pretty fishy when the Wit would go out on trips and parties with them, without me knowing. Yes, a very strong fishy stench indeed and it wasn't the expired garoupa I was talking about.

To add salt to the wound, he was quite a man about town as well. In clubs, when most guys would be contented in strutting their stuff on the dance floor, not Olivier. Donned with eye-blinding bling-blings, he had to be on stage or some visibly clear space where he could be the center of the universe.

Ladies and gentlemen, the ego has landed.

Excuse me flashy, but the podium is only for ladies and I don't see any tits on you so scram. That smug look on his face that time.

Tsk tsk Something tells me he was lapping up the attention like a beagle to a puddle of water. You can never trust a funnyman dad used to say. Wait, that was a good looking man. Bah, it's the same.

Olivier also bore a tattoo on his arm. Yes, we all know you underwent tremendous torture when Brute was scraping your skin and poking you with a sharp pointy instrument, we share your pain. But can you for once put on something else other than your sleeveless tees? We are in the middle of a freak storm for heaven's sake!

Did I mention Mr. Comedy a.k.a. Mr. Flamboyant drove an ostentatious sports car as well? Yes he did. What is this with men and cars anyway? I did not mind that he owned a big boy's toy. It was pretty cool I must admit. But did he have to honk at every girl he saw on the road? Hello....some sensitivity here please! Initially I thought it was a silly prank to make me laugh. I threw that notion out of his car window when he started stopping beside unknown girls to flirt with them – with me in the car still.

It was also becoming quite a spectacle and a bit of a nuisance during my outings with him. He'd be holding my hand while concurrently chatting up 5-6 girls standing around us giggling silly at his wisecracks.

Writing this section on Olivier made me remember all the photos that we took together. It either depicted him pointing to some imaginary object from afar, or him lifting something heavy be it a rock, a dog or sometimes me. And I mean ALL the photos. The motive was simple: all these poses would clearly show off his somewhat rippling biceps and the 4 packs that he had painstakingly sculpted. "Sorry babe, but can you stand just a wee further back? You are blocking the sun from shining onto my face."

My funny friend had been a flashy freak in hiding all this while. Suddenly I did not find him amusing anymore. He became public property whilst I, public enemy number one. The girls simply adored him and would eliminate any living thing that stood in their way. And the Wit was enjoying himself silly.

I'm too sexy for my love alright.

I think it was during that defining moment, when Olivier was dancing and being sandwiched between 2 sets of heaving boobs that I told him "You know Olivier, I thought we could make it. But I reckoned Boobsie and Tootsie here will do a better job in keeping you happy. By the way, your hairline is receding."

Goodbyes can be so bittersweet.

Reflection: I want to put the record straight here by saying I have nothing against funny men. However, there exist various categories of funny, where the guy can either tickle the girl senseless, or make her want to stuff giant marshmallows in her ears. My keen sense of observation skills (i.e. people watching at shopping malls and parties) have enabled me to come up with the following categories: -

To all the aspiring funny guys, please take heed.

Category 1: Natural comedians

While some people are born with a silver spoon in their mouths, these guys are born with a 100 extra set of funny bones, 1 for each girl they date. Give them 5 seconds and they can spin a funny story out of anything......right down to the tub of yoghurt that has gone bad. They make you laugh so hard, you roll down on the floor not because of stomach cramps, but to desperately stop yourself from wetting your panties. *Yup, they work their laughs so effortlessly; you'll gladly denounce your religion and sell your nanna just to get another quip from them.*

Category 2: The-Try-Too-Hards

You can hear them a mile away. They will be the ones laughing the loudest at their own jokes, while everyone else is still digesting what they said. Their anecdotes are indeed quite hilarious.....that is until you discover it was all recycled from the latest edition of the 1001 Jokes book. Whilst you should forgive them for these desperate attempts at funnydom, their inclination towards creating puns that borders the offensive will jolly well make you want to scratch your fingernails against the blackboard just to soothe your assaulted ears.

Category 3: Awkward wannabes

Their comic tales are usually received by blank stares and wide mouths a gaped. Either that or the whole room hushes down into a you-can-hear-a-pin-drop silence, only to be broken by sounds of nervous laughter from the narrator and his frantically darting eyes. Poor guys, they just want to be funny. But their quips can be so obscure, I'm afraid only Martians get them. Maybe the next one buddy.

It is okay to date a funnyman, but be wary of which group they are lumped under. Ensure the wit does not come with oversized ego that can't even squeeze through the front door, or takes pleasure in telling the most offensive and unforgivably bad anecdotes. If thrown in such situations, advised to chuck the funny boy and retreat immediately.

HONEY, I HAVE SOMETHING TO TELL YOU

Cupid struck again after a few months' hiatus.

My fateful encounter with T.J occurred on a typical night out with friends at a favorite watering hole. My first impressions upon meeting this considerably attractive looking guy were these thoughts "Okay, no signs of over inflated ego and no inkling of secret aspirations to be an assassin". My interest has definitely been piqued.

"GASP". Will he be the one that will actually free me from the seemingly inescapable curse of "You shall only date Weird and Regrettable Men"?

I'm also pretty sure his chiseled face, toned physique and his skillful ways with the ladies did not contribute much to my instant gravitation towards him. Alright, let us not kid ourselves. I was close to dropping on my knees, throwing my arms up in the air and shouting "Hallelujah!" for behold, stood before me was actually a normal (with some good looks thrown in) guy! I shall not be plagued by sob stories no more! Joy to the world.....

Things were honky dory in the beginning, and it was like a breath of fresh air for me. I did not have to fear T.J would be lurking around in my backyard after dark, or having my ears audibly battered from listening to another cheesy pick up line.

I also did not find it odd that more often than not we'd bump into one of his girl friends that seemed to have shared a 'history' with him. Perhaps he was popular with the girls with his helplessly charming self? Or maybe the girls themselves were the ones which relentlessly pursued him like a pack of hungry wolves? Yes, that must be it. But whatever the truth was, I chose to be ignorantly in bliss. So what if he had a colorful past? Mine was not entirely white as a sheet either. I thought I had finally nabbed myself a promising guy, free of major defects. Dammit, I was very well hanging on to this one!

Casual dinners after work, aimless strolls inside shopping centers, partying at the latest clubs and catching the occasional movies at the cinema: these were the seemingly mundane activities which to me were a welcomed change. Six months down the road and no signs of trouble yet. Not the glaring ones at least. Sure, his mood swings at times swung frantically like a pendulum a few times a day. I wasn't going to rock the boat, and in all honesty he was so much saner compared to his predecessors. As long as there was nothing overtly wrong with him, I'll take him - lock, stock and barrel!

If I could have a penny for every time a woman tells me how they have settled for someone that was just remotely better than their crazy ex, I would be whizzing around town in my yellow Beetle now.

Instead of steadfastly searching for their Mr. Right, most jaded women end up rationalizing and convincing themselves that Mr. Right Now is not entirely that bad. I call this the Knight in Kind of Shining Armor Syndrome.

Don't get me wrong, I am not claiming all Mr. Right Now's are women's' momentarily lapse of judgment, and that they will forever be stamped as first runner ups. There are lots of happy cases where the Right Now's morphed into Rights in the end. All I am saying is that I commiserate with them in some cases, especially when the woman knows she is settling for second best, and her intuition is blaring with all these warning signals to get out.

In essence they are entering into a very risky relationship, as what happens when Mr. Right appears later in her life? Or worst, the couple end up bickering and squabbling about everything under the sun? Scram right now or don't-you-dare-touch-me would sound more like it by then.

Some women might break out in a protest right about now yelling "Bah! There's no such thing as Mr. Right! Blame it on those conniving movie and music producers for deluding our minds." Now just hold on to your skirt there missy. If we perhaps set realistic expectations on what constitutes The One for us, maybe, just maybe he won't be so elusive anymore and might just be sitting right under your nose all this time.

Anyway, I digress; now back to T.J and I.

Gut feelings. Never underestimate this powerful internal sensor. After all, it has been imbedded in us for a good reason. It's like when you are grocery shopping and the butcher tries to sell his last piece of sirloin to you. You poke at the meat, give it a quick sniff and poke at it again. No reaction whatsoever from the slab. Gut feelings will tell you to switch to chicken chop that night.

I knew something wasn't quite right when during an uneventful night after work, T.J said he was coming over to my place. He arrived at my apartment, and asked to talk to me privately in my bedroom. I remember the air-conditioner was switched on as very soon it would have made me feel as if I was in Antarctica. He proceeded to ask me to stay calm and he took in a big nervous gulp before uttering "Honey, I have something to tell you." The ensuing chain of events became a blurry scene afterwards.

I vividly recall him asking me about whether I remember that he met up with one of his long lost friends a few days ago. He also asked me whether I recalled they shared a 'history' together. Yes to both. The story went that after having dinner, she broke the news to him that she had in fact given birth to their child – one year ago.

Choir: FIGAROH, FIGAROH, FIGAROH, FIGAROOOOH! (*this opera song is usually played during a suspenseful turn of events in my favorite Bugs Bunny cartoons.*)

Whoooa…..what? Did I just get sucked into the Twilight Zone? How was this possible? You think he would have known if he had a son, right? And that he would have told me at the start of our courtship, right? What was all this psycho babble?

I found my body shivering in the suddenly freezing air, and I thought I had lost partial hearing abilities as everything else was pretty much a mumble to me after the dropping of that bombshell.

My very first thought was whether this was his attempt at a very twisted joke. Upon detecting his solemn face, the next thing that

came to my mind was, "Yikes"! I am now bearer of a very foul title -
the Other woman. Yesterday, I was his legitimate girlfriend. Today,
I felt like I was having an illicit affair with this guy who has a child
and a 'wife'. I had become the accidental dirty mistress.

My Knight in Kind of Shining Armor had transformed into a
Greek tragedy personified. Pavlovas and meatballs began to swirl
mercilessly in my head, and I was close to smashing the new set of
China in my next door neighbor's cupboard.

The feeling of desolation that gripped me then started to slowly
evaporate. All of a sudden, a sense of peace swept across me. I
just knew what I had to do. I told him I'm stepping out from the
relationship as I just couldn't picture myself wrecking his new found
family.

I wish I could make everyone proud by concluding that I then
went off with my head held high. But the next few weeks after that
conversation saw me plummeting into a near emotional chasm. Was
he telling me the truth? Was it a cheap and fast shot to break off with
me? Had he known all this while? I was very close to asking for a
DNA test as proof. Just make sure you take a few jabs at his nether
region to get that blood sample nurse.

It took me a good few months before I gained real perspective
on the duration that we were going out. Truth was I had already
noticed big cracks in our courtship earlier on. Nonetheless, I chose
to desperately patch these cracks up even though I knew it was
shoddy work, and focused on whatever good points that was left.
The incident, as perplexing as it was had acted as a wake-up call
for me to accept the demise of a relationship that was never really
meant to be.

Reflections: My biggest lesson from this saga was that things happen for a reason. I know, I know, it sounds very cliché but it's true. Think about it. If events and experiences (the good, bad and ugly) do not happen as planned, then the whole world will be in total chaos wouldn't it? I'm also a believer that we are all somehow intricately linked to one another, intertwined with experiences that have a cause and effect correlation between all inhabitants of Earth. Okay okay, bordering New Age talk there but you know what I mean.

In retrospect, I already had this feeling right down to the cockles of my heart that we weren't meant together. It was just a matter of time, and a matter of which one of us would be the bad guy to actually end it. My feelings of desolation after our breakup wasn't due to losing the biggest love of my life, but rather the mourning of the sudden, abrupt ending of a relationship that quite frankly may have ended a long time ago.

Before one decides to wail in self pity after a breakup, look at the relationship in hindsight and ask yourself whether this was a blessing in disguise.

Could you have seen your unborn children in his eyes? Would it have been utterly blissful if his face was the first thing you see every morning and every night, for every single day of your life til death do you part?! If thoughts like these are sending uncontrollable shivers through your spine and causing you to break out in a cold sweat, something tells me you are better off without him.

CONTRIBUTIONS FROM THE ROMANTICALLY CHALLENGED

Contributor's info: Chloe, 29, next top film producer, Malaysia
Ex category: Virtual infatuation
Story: Narrated by author

Chloe was a late bloomer in the boys department. She spent a good twenty years equating boys with being smelly, rough and having an incomprehensible obsession towards fast cars and blood-spattered sports. She thought they were creatures from another universe, and had no idea why her girl friends were going positively gaga over them. "Explain to me again why you find hairy arms and smelly armpits so attractive?" she would quiz with semi-sarcasm.

Mention the word grooming to her, and you'll be at the receiving end of a loud huff at this so called 'blasphemy'. It was at this period as well that Chloe boldly embarked on a one-girl act of protest by refusing to comb her hair and snubbing skirts and all things frilly. She proudly paraded a tee with the words 'Boys are stupid, throw rocks at them' around town. That controversial attire nearly sparked a new rebellion, if not for it mysteriously 'disappearing' in the washer and never to be seen again.

There were a few brave souls that tried to thaw her from her cool exterior. But her piercing glares and threats to bite succeeded in sending those innocent guys running home with their tail between their legs.

Then one day, puberty hit her like a windscreen to a fly.

It happened at the ripe age of 21, and her hormones were finally jolted awake from their prolonged slumber.

Chloe began to notice guys around her. "Hmm, what is this tingling sensation I'm feeling whenever a guy looks at me? Not only does their armpit doesn't seem to bother me anymore, but I'm actually intrigued by the musky smell it's emitting. Holy cow, I must be going nuts".

Chloe's long-awaited puberty finally arrived, and at that same time a little technological invention called the Internet came blasting into our lives. Overnight, cyber cafes mushroomed in every corner and Internet chat rooms began hanging on the lips of every Internet savvy person.

Chloe stumbled into this whole new realm of online (in lack of a better word) meat market, and not long after that found herself bearing nicknames such as 'Cutesy Poo' and 'Buttercup88' chatting excitingly with mysterious guys from around the globe. What a far cry from the boys are stupid days.

During one typical A/S/L chat, Chloe met a guy I shall term Lee. He appeared down to earth, funny and trustworthy. And she had a good inkling he wasn't an old hermit or a pimplish adolescent masquerading as a twenty-something year old.

It was still too early to meet in person so they resorted to the second best alternative – phone chats. Chloe was exhilarated to finally put a voice behind her Arial text and smiley faces. She gladly left the rest of her to Lee's vivid imagination.

Chatting on the internet had progressed to chatting on the phone. And the innocent pre-dinner conversations were quickly replaced by midnight exchanges over the phone.

One night, Chloe's roommate Debbie was awakened in her sleep by the sounds of whispering and giggling. She laid still whilst she listened intently to the quiet singing that was now taking place. Was she dreaming? She opened one eye to scan the room and almost let out a loud snicker. Chloe was crouching underneath her table and singing into her mobile phone. Debbie's once tomboyish friend has finally mastered the art of flirting. In the dead of the night too mind you.

Chloe added a whole new dimension to duet-ing. The serenade went something like this….

Chloe: Oh….my love….my darling, I've hungered for your touch….(giggle giggle).

Lee: Aaaaaaiiiiii neeeeed your love (shriek, hit the wrong note).

Chloe: Oh….I need…..your love….. (long sigh).

Lee: Godspeed your love to meeee (shriek, another wrong note and quick gasp).

Unchained Melody never sounded so……..wistful. And it sent goose bumps and shivers down Debbie's body. She went back to sleep with her hands covering her mouth, in case she burst out laughing and rudely interrupting the romantic duet.

These midnight rendezvous continued for about one month, before Lee finally made the proposal to meet.

Chloe was a bit hesitant as she has heard one too many horror stories about these moments of final revelation. One of her close friends almost reached a state of euphoria when she and her virtual beau decided to meet. She flaunted his picture of a tall, dark and handsome figure to everyone she knew and was certain she had bagged herself a clear winner.

Tall, dark and handsome turned out to be a balding, bloating pervert with a few missing teeth thrown in. She reminded herself to have some words with the creators of Photoshop.

The meet up was close to being unbearable, and she made a mad dash out of the restaurant when he went to the loo. It wasn't his constant salivating or him picking his nose midway through his appetizer that irked her. The last straw came when he ogled a few inches too low below her neckline and smugly asked "So, am I everything you expected?"

Shrugging that nightmare off, Chloe decided she just had to meet her masked duet partner. She prepped herself mentally for the worst that could happen. "If need be, I can always feign a case of bad diarrhea. My flatulence can finally be put to good use," she convinced herself.

With that in mind, the Big day finally arrived.

Armed with a grainy picture of Lee that he emailed over just the night before, Chloe arrived at their meeting place – a café in one of the shopping malls in town. She felt her stomach churning and wasn't quite sure whether it was the questionable curry she ate that morning or her jitters. She popped in and out of the ladies for like ten times to make sure that darn stray hair stayed in its place.

When she finally approached the café, she quickly dived behind a wall when she caught a glimpse of a guy that resembled Lee. "Okay, breathe in, breathe out. Here goes nothing."

Chloe put on her biggest smile and in her best nonchalant manner started approaching Lee. "I wonder if he'll drop to his knees and break into a rendition of My Girl," she wondered. She conjured up an image of both of them singing hand in hand and tap dancing out of the mall towards the sunset, with bluebirds lining their path. Chloe quickly snapped out of her daydream and checked her hair for that one last time.

At last they came face to face, and after a few seconds of held breaths and skipped heartbeats, finally exchanged the cordial hellos and broke out in nervous laughter.

Lee wasn't that bad after all. It was indeed his face in the picture, and true enough his personality mimicked his online character. And Chloe was quite certain that Lee felt she lived up to her descriptions as he hasn't come up with a lame excuse to split from the scene.

Yet, they found it hard to actually hold a conversation that lasted for more than one minute. Compared to their online chats that sometimes made them missed their meals and calls of nature, now in the flesh they were at lost for words. They even attempted to create a topic about the checkered tablecloth on their table and thought it may be fun to count the number of boxes in it. Thirty minutes into this 'exciting' act, Lee said he forgot to bathe his dog. Coincidentally Chloe developed an unexpected case of stomach upset. They both made their own quick exit.

Truth be told, the magic went poof the day they both met. Lee was like the rabbit that has been yanked out from the hat. Most of the allure of engaging in a virtual relationship is the element of surprise and shrouded mystery. Now that reality has bunked off mystery, Lee no longer appeared to be that appealing.

The night time serenades dwindled down, and Chloe's meal times and bathrooms visits went back to a normal routine. She still chats to Lee occasionally on the Internet, but in a very cordial fashion. There was nothing naughty or forbidden about their liaison anymore. No more guessing about how he really is or what he really looks like in real life. Chloe's fantasy was quenched and now Lee seemed like any normal guy. The two slowly drifted apart and Chloe has not been involved in another midnight sing-a-long since.

Reflections: It is not everyone's cup of tea to meet eligible partners on the World Wide Web. The aspect of not knowing who you're really talking to either gives you a sense of addictive pleasure or conversely makes you ponder which nutcase is on the other side.

You really have to have a good distinction between infatuation and what is right smack real. It is quite thrilling to be able to meet countless guys at the touch of your fingertips. But what happens when the dream is ousted by reality? Is there enough substance in these relationships for them to step up to the next level?

I'm sure a majority of women will have no whims at all, save for the handful that stubbornly insists in clinging on to their image of perfection (even after the guy has manifested himself, with or without defects). For the latter, a kind Samaritan will just have to slap them back into the real world.

But there's no denying that Internet chat rooms have proven to be quite a powerful mingling place, and in some cases leading to saying "I Do's" between these Internet-spawned couples. Provided we can clearly distinguish the line that separates online romanticism from the offline world, the Internet may just be the best matchmaking tool in the 21st century.

Contributor's info: Lindy Lou, 27, future domestic goddess, Australia
Ex category: Mixed nuts – medley of botched tales

The Body

Once upon a time I met this guy called Mark. He was the epitome of sexy. His muscular body was a lean mean body building machine. Plainly put it, he was finger-licking gorgeous.

His profession was of course nothing short of manly; I think it was mechanical engineering, construction or something along those brawny lines. Heck, I was just too busy ogling at him. Whatever that came out from his mouth didn't really matter much to me.

In fact, our initial meeting didn't involve any talking at all. I saw him on the dance floor and I was instantly hooked like a fish to a worm. Before I knew it I got involved in a bit of a body-grinding action on the dance floor. My friends were aghast as I always had been the "quiet and sensible one". Of course at the time I didn't care because my brain took a backseat and my hormones took over.

I don't think you could call the courtship with Mark 'dating'. We spent more time kissing than talking. However, when we did stop for air I noticed that his accent was incredibly thick. Most foreign accents are charming but his was far, far from it. To be really kind to him, he sounded like a donkey with a nasal problem. English was as foreign to him as eating burgers with beetroot. There was one time when he said "I want to go to the dentist" and I nodded enthusiastically as I thought he said "I want to buy you pressies".

Snow-boarding was one of his many obsessions. His goal in life was to work in Canada as a ski-lift operator. He reasoned that this would allow him to snowboard during his time off. Shucks, don't we all love guys with ambition?

His other fixation was talking about his ex-girlfriend. She had dumped him two years ago but he would speak about it as if it happened last month. Our daily conversations were like a broken recorder with the incessant playing and replaying of Mark's account of his pitiful breakup.

As I was hypnotized by his amazing body, none of these flaws bothered me. I figured he was a real good catch and I was happy to spend the rest of my life with him. Brains, brawns....what's the difference? But he, on the other hand, thought otherwise and a few weeks later gave me the most ungracious flick. I was heartbroken. Luckily I was young with a very short attention span and got over him in a few weeks' time.

Reflections: From this brief relationship I learnt that having an eye-candy is a lot of fun, but the fun is usually short lived. It doesn't help either when he keeps mumbling about bringing you pressies, when in reality he wanted to go to the dentist instead. So for those of you who are thinking of having a little fling with a brainless hunk of a man, beware – as you may find yourself wanting to wring his neck rather than nuzzle it!

The Pretty boy

A good girlfriend of mine was smitten by this guy called Nathan. Soon I was acting as her side-kick with her dragging me by the hair to every function and party that he would appear. He was indeed a very pretty boy and all the girls would talk about how cute he was. I wasn't impressed because he was just a tad bit shy from looking like a girl himself. He had a fringe that partly covered his obscenely long eye lashes and possessed the smoothest complexion. I really didn't know Snow White had a brother.

It had taken a whole year for my friend to realize that he wasn't going to ask her out, let alone propose to her. So eventually, I stopped getting dragged along and I no longer saw him at all. However, one day I bumped into Nathan by accident and I discovered that this pretty boy had a pretty good sense of humor. He somehow convinced me to come along with him to a dancing class and between the swinging from waltz to cha-cha he asked me out on a date.

At first everything was nice and sweet. He loved holding my hands and whispering romantic things to me. He was full of surprises as well, like when he led me to a special spot and we gazed at the stars. He even asked me to name one of the stars after me so we could both remember it forever. Pretty boy sure had his ways with the ladies.

However I was getting a little impatient. When was the first kiss ever going to happen? Come on and just plant me a wet one now. Several dates later, he finally made his move. After dinner one night, over a cup of hot chocolate, Nathan ever so slowly started to lean towards me with his lips pursed. I waited for the long awaited kiss but nothing happened. I pried open one eye to find him still working out the correct angle to tilt his head. I waited a few more minutes as I was sure with a face like that he was going to be a darn good kisser. By the time I felt a slight peck on the lips I was on the verge of death by boredom. He on the other hand was over the moon; that was his first kiss you see.

Even though he was very shy with the smooching bits, I found that he was not at all bashful about checking himself out. Before every outing, he would come out and ask me, "So how do I look?" or he would stop and check his hair every time he passed anything that showed his reflection. He even gave me a photo of himself to put into my wallet. Of course it was of him standing there in his "I'm Mr. Beautiful" stance with the wind blowing through his hair. To top things off, I realized his voice could get really whiny especially when he laughed. It would sound very similar to a hyena in labor. I stopped making any jokes, in case he might laugh unnecessarily.

Two months later I called it quits.

Reflection: I learnt that there are plenty of men out there who are much vainer than women. It has become so common to see guys strutting around wearing lip gloss and carrying man-bags. Take heed though, as there's a huge lot of difference between being metrosexual and plain conceited. And I can safely vouch that most girls would prefer their guys not be the main hogger of mirrors.

And I also learnt that laughter in a relationship is really important. Your partner's laughter should resonate like music to your years, not like a screeching cat being splashed by a bucket of cold water.

The Traditional guy

I never imagined I would go out with a guy 7 years older than me. In fact, I didn't find out his age until after our first date and by then I was already starting to fall for him. We met at a barbeque while I was waiting for the sausages to defrost. He was very funny and easy going.

Greg and I went out and things went smoothly. He was young at heart and he was also very soft-hearted. Being a karate instructor, he was both strong and sturdy and was a lot more responsible and grown up than I was then. I felt like I was always looked after. However, I soon realized that he had something up his sleeves and it wasn't ready cooked sausages that sealed our fate.

He envisioned that in the future I would stay at home, slaving away to do the cooking and cleaning. Being a very ambitious young lady, culinary skills were not part of my forte. Even boiling eggs proved to be quite a challenge to me. He also wanted me to learn to cook and master all his favorite meals from his own mother. I hadn't even met his mother, but from what he told me his whole family hated me even though they hadn't met me. I'm guessing they found out about the egg-boiling incident (or lack thereof).

Naturally all my friends hated him. They were waiting for me to dump him. But it didn't turn out that way at all. I was completely naïve at the time and I was optimistic that one day his demands would just go away. "I'll slowly wean him off his mother's milk and replace it with Colonel Sanders" I would tell them. One year later he dumped me because I still couldn't tell the difference between spatulas and tarantulas.

Reflections: This was my first-hand experience of having someone attempting to change me. It was a little bit scary and proved to be quite fruitless really. Women are like ginger, it gets harder (and more fiery?) as it gets older.

So for those of you who are trying to change your partner, think twice as it'll likely be a futile task. If you like your partner, you have to accept their strengths and weaknesses - egg boiling abilities and all.

<u>Mama's Boy</u>

I finally found a boy named Jeremy who spoke perfectly good English, wasn't too vain and didn't expect me to cook, ever. It seemed my prayers were finally answered. I met him at university. I was with one of my classmates and we were running away from one of our other classmates whom we did not want to sit with for lunch. She happened to be quite irritating, constantly keeping the class back late because of her incessant questions. Unfortunately she found us and she brought along a friend which happened to be Jeremy.

Jeremy often told funny stories during lunch and we would see him every week. I didn't pay too much attention though because I was too busy scoffing my lunch down whilst scrambling to get my homework done for the next class. Two years later, my course was completed and I started to work. He had kept in touch with me throughout that time. From being mere lunch time partners we ascended to a status of a couple.

It was truly great at first. As he was close to my age, his friends were easy to get along with. He was entertaining to talk to and we were comfortable spending all our time together.

But all this changed after the mother came into the picture.

Don't get me wrong, she was a pleasant woman and was kind and caring. However she loved her only boy fiercely and needed to know where he was, what he was doing and who he was with 24/7. "Boy, are you coming home for dinner? Don't forget our dinner times on Friday, Saturday and Sunday okay. And remember your handkerchief before you go out."

He thought this was completely normal and couldn't understand why I hated the sound of his ringing mobile. He loved his mother dearly and couldn't see the problem of being mothered around at the ripe age of 25. When he was a university student, his mom would drive him to and fro campus. This pattern continued well into his working life with his mom driving him to the train station to go to work. She would listen to his concerns and cheer him up when he was in a lousy mood.

I soon found that the trend followed on with me. He thought it was perfectly fine to use my car instead of buying his own. He was often in a lousy mood and I spent plenty of nights talking him out of it and patting his head as he rested it on my bosoms. I also discovered that he loved hearing the sound of his own voice. He would often re-tell a story for the 100th time, even after with me politely telling him that I've already heard it. He would pause for a second, passed me a blank stare and resumed with his narration.

Four and a half years later, I came to my senses and worked out that being single suited me better.

Reflections: Having the multiple roles of a girlfriend cum counselor cum driver is really exhausting work. Of course we should take pride in our instinctive nature to nurture, but we need to draw the line somewhere! Like the saying goes, spare the rod and spoil the child. No good letting the guy latch on to you for motherly support as then he will never break out from his cocoon.

Contributor's info: Bo Bette, 35, banker, Malaysia
Duration of courtship: What courtship?
Ex category: Liar Liar Pants on Fire

Having just parted ways with my last partner of 9 months, my happily attached girlfriends banded together and decided they carried a civic duty to start match making me with eligible bachelors. Alright, I was just being nice – the reality was that they took great delight in introducing me to anyone that resembled a normal guy just to see whether we would hit it off. Whack a pair of khakis on a fire hydrant and they probably would have set us up on a blind date. "He's just a bit shy" would have been their excuse.

After what seemed like an eternity of coaxing, I finally gave in and agreed to be their guinea pig. Furthermore, the last time I resisted they threatened to stop making me my favorite cupcakes. There was just too much at stake.

Isaiah met me at a coffee club the very next day. Nothing was going to shock me as I went in holding a very low expectation about this character that my friends convinced me was a great catch. Hmm, that was exactly the same thing they promised me when they shoved Mr. I Know Everything to my face last year.

Isaiah appeared sociable and chatty, and was thoughtful enough to give me a self-made ceramic mug that he just so happened to have an extra one on hand (this would be his first lie). Scrappy and whatever goes would be how I'd illustrated his outlook – wanton hair that desperately needed to be trimmed, shirts that dated back to the

70's and shoes that I think would look more flattering on his dad. But hey, I wasn't expecting us to be anything more than friends so with no trouble I bypassed all of that.

I slowly learned that he was an up and coming producer in the film industry and began impressing me with stories about his multi-million dollar projects in Asia and cutting the latest deals in the US (still unverified). Back then I hardly knew any guy that was in the creative business. He got my near hardened creative juices flowing again as we discussed about an experimental movie we could do together. Note that I never had the intention of treating him as my boyfriend. I also made it clear to him that it would be strictly business between us, in which he agreed. My womanly instincts told me otherwise but I was too engrossed at the potential of realizing my long awaited Loofah and Scrubs film with this rare artistic whiz.

We would proceed to meet up quite regularly after that to discuss about our new endeavor. I even managed to rope in some of my other friends to add to the creative mixture that was now brewing excitingly. I did find it peculiar then on how he used to supposingly come up with the greatest ideas around midnight and insisted that I met up with him. We'd spend about 10 minutes on his 'ideas' where the rest of the night would see him confiding in me some of the most intimate details about his personal life – unsolicited.

This did not preclude him sharing with me his cousin's latest surgery on the most delicate part of her body. There was definitely no holds barred as he enthusiastically described to me the end-to-end medical procedure and making sure no slimy details were left out. I was midway through sipping my tomato juice, but decided to leave it for fear of me having to partake in some projectile vomiting thus making a mess of myself. I forced a smile when he finished narrating while at the same moment praying very hard that what I've just heard would not traumatize me too badly.

Isaiah also thought by repeating to me again and again about the girl he last dated would be of interest to me. Like a broken recorder, he would lament about how she toyed with his feelings, used up most of his hard-earned money and made him her part-time chauffer. He had no reservations referring to her as the slut or tramp and after every account his face would turn bright red with vehemence. Alright, that was nice but can we get back to our pet project now?

Reflecting back, I think in some odd way that was him having a crack at forging a closer bond with me. Little did he know that all that time I was thinking of one word that would come to describe him fittingly: Cuckoo. I blame his smart idiot friends that taught him these disastrous moves.

I became suspicious about Isaiah's true motives when a few months went by with our mini production still up in the air. We have spent countless hours discussing about it and promises after promises were made by him in rounding up his movie-making friends and preparing the first shoot. All that started to sound like plain old lip service to me.

His real intentions began to creep up like a worm out of its hole. During one meeting, I answered his mobile phone while he stepped out for a while. By a stroke of 'luck' I stumbled upon his images file where to my horror found numerous pictures of me, all taken without my knowledge or consent for that matter. To make it worst, this was stored inside the same folder that contained pictures of semi-naked women in the most suggestive poses.

When he came back, I made sure I was going to squeeze some answers out of him. "You better sing like a canary or else I'll be introducing you to Salib, my muscular and menacing friend." For my secretly snapped shots, he admitted that he wanted us to be more than friends. He was even planning to create a collage out of all those photos that he had slyly taken of me. As for his other collections, his alibi was that his phone had been ruthlessly hacked and the perpetrator had downloaded those dirty pictures without him knowing. Which really begs the next question of why he was still retaining them then?

That was positively one of the fluffiest excuses I have ever heard in my life.

My qualms about the distorted one were further confirmed upon learning from a common friend that Isaiah tricked him into discussing a potential lucrative deal one afternoon, only to be locked up for half a day being forced to divulge every bit of information about me.

I resolved to steer clear from this phony and reluctantly stowed my manuscript back into the drawers. There is still some hope of me bumping into Spielberg right? This will not be the last of Loofahs and Scrubs people.

But that was not the last I heard or saw of Isaiah. I would see him turning up at almost every event that I was at, and when queried about his presence he would casually label it as pure coincidence. I honestly imagined he had snuck inside my office and stole my calendar and who knows what else.

The scariest incident would have to be my 25th birthday, a month after I ended our 'joint venture'. He sent me a present which I thought was a peace offering. I was all ready to let bygones be bygones when he called me that same night asking whether I have opened the present. I said not as yet, but I thanked him for his nice gesture.

The whole ground shook and rumbled beneath my feet – akin to the calm before the storm that was about to befall on us. As if he was possessed he started berating and hollering at me. "Why didn't you open the present when you got it? Don't you like what I've given you? It's a pair of stuffed giraffes and a pair of hand-sewn pillows you thankless woman!"

I was holding my breath both in utter shock and half expecting him to charge like a rhino at my bedroom door. I honestly couldn't tell whether all the tranquilizers in the vicinity could have subdued that raging animal then. I got ready to retort back and give him a large piece of my mind when he got off the line. Lucky him.

The next morning, after recovering from that ghastly conversation, I discovered that Isaiah had circulated an email to all of my friends duly informing them about the heinous 'crime' I had committed. It was simply unacceptable that I did not open his present the second I received it and immediately expressed my gratitude for him, which clearly implied that I was ungrateful and unabashed. He demanded for justice to be done and rallied my friends to stand behind him in this grave matter.

No need to mention here that my friends immediately wrote him off as a nutcase.

Isaiah epitomized the kind of guy that really shouldn't be allowed to date. Surely there were more than a dozen loose screws in that head! I should have flung him inside the loony bin a long time ago. With his brains and creativity he was like a twisted predator out to create mayhem on unwary women's lives. Deep down inside me I was so very extremely glad we never became partners, be it in the business or personal space. I don't know how long I could've endured before I made him into a stuffed animal myself.

Reflections: It is so easy for women in general to be attracted to the artistic cum unusual sorts. Their creative nature and unique perception of the world paints such a much more interesting picture of the same humdrum place that we live in.

However, I should have known from the start that there was something up nutcase's dodgy sleeves. I guess I was partly to be blamed for brushing aside my instincts and pretending we could just have been friends. It was also so much less of a conundrum to attribute his obvious lies and weird behavior to his innate eccentric self, when I knew very well there was something seriously wrong with the man!

I was refusing to let my dreams go down the drains, and thought bearing with his deceit was a reasonable tradeoff in realizing one of my ambitions. In short, I almost shortchanged myself and boy was I glad I came out with some coins left still!

But you know what? Nothing is worth making us lie to ourselves or being lied to or being subjected to crazy accusations. Who said we needed to depend on others to make our dreams come true? If we put our whole mind and heart into it, there's really nothing we can't accomplish.

Contributor's info: Veronica, in her thirties, entrepreneur, Singapore
Duration of courtship: Too long
Ex category: Who's your Daddy?

Jingle bells, jingle bells, jingle all the way....la la la.

I met Nathaniel at church during a pre-Christmas concert. Nothing happened the first time we met as we chatted with others about the morning's sermon, and then moving on to a more enticing discussion about the latest skits on Seinfeld.

Most people will agree that while gaining spiritual enlightenment is undoubtedly the main aim in attending these places of worship, let us be totally frank and admit there's a large number of people (if not all of the singles) go there in hope of hooking up with someone nice as well. Absolutely nothing wrong with that second agenda as long as we've got our priorities right, right?

Anyway, where was I? Oh yes, Nathaniel.

When I got to know him, I had just moved to a new state and was diligently scouring the job market for work. Four months came and gone and my main occupation then was still counting the flies that circled around the stale loaf of bread. I was starting to get worried about paying my next month's rent, and was psyching myself up on the possibility of selling my favorite woolen coat.

It must have been my vulnerability and a hint of loneliness where the next thing I knew I was having kung-pow beef at his home and getting cozy with his parents (also partly because the hole in my purse was doubling in its size). "Nathaniel should be a pretty harmless beau. You can't really go wrong with a God-fearing man," I thought.

Some of goody-goody two shoe's plus points were that he exuded a very tranquil, articulate and gentlemanly persona. If he was bitten by a snake, without a hitch he would calmly capture the reptile before hopping to the nearest vet for help. Of course throughout the journey he'd be telling the snake what a naughty-naughty boy it had been.

He held a brief stint as a kindergarten teacher when he was working overseas, and I must say it trained him well. He would speak to me as if I was a precious child, slotting in praises and compliments after almost every sentence. I can vouch for all women when I say we simply love to be nurtured. Goo goo ga ga.

But there was no question about it; Nathaniel's deep throaty voice was my biggest downfall. Whatever he said I'd be almost hypnotized by it. He could have told me to lick a lollipop and I'll say "What flavor?"

His protective figure made me feel secure and taken care of, like a mother hen to its chick. I started noticing myself checking to see that I sat upright, didn't fidget around and chewed with my mouth closed whenever he was around. There is always room for good manners.

Nathaniel also began to slowly wean me off from my occasional harmless outings to dance clubs. Attending friends' hen's nights were also barred. I was almost sure that he was about to reinstate a curfew for me, but for whatever reason decided to postpone that action.

I also had to adhere to a very strict dress code whenever I went out with him. There was one time when we were in a lift, and one of my bra straps accidentally slid off my shoulder. With a very solemn face he looked at it and said "You may want to adjust that back up again and make that tighter". I was instantly transported back to when I was 7 and was reprimanded for eating during class.

My friends were not spared as well from his lashing as they recounted the time they got into a pretty heated argument with him when they were planning for my upcoming birthday celebration. My ever adventurous girlfriends wanted to take me on a 'Wild Boys Afloat' cruise but Nathaniel vetoed that idea unilaterally. According to him, that "immoral form of entertainment" would corrupt my innocent mind and soul. And they would be no different from the devil's advocates if they insisted on this blasphemes act.

It was highly fortunate that this argument transpired on emails, else I had no doubt he would be the recipient of some karate chops and Thai boxing kicks.

As for talking to other male species, he would almost always cast his steely eyes on me like a hawk, watching my every move. I had stopped being chummy with them, and didn't even dare think about giving them a friendly peck on the cheek or a goodbye hug. No need to put them through another round of unwarranted scolding.

Your mind must be boggling right about now as to how I failed to notice any of these warning signs. I want to say they had evaded me in such a conniving way, but then I'd be lying. Truth was, he acted as my security blanket and also I was getting used to him tucking me into bed at night.

I was going through the pressures of the job hunting game and was also living far away from home. I regarded him as my surrogate family. You can be forgiven to think he was quite stern and harsh especially when I committed a boo boo, but a little smack on my hands were just part of making me a better person, won't you agree?

I think someone up there took pity on me when during one grocery shopping trip, I chanced upon him crossing the road. I just froze in my tracks and started feeling all my senses flooding back into me when I saw him in one of the most unimaginable acts. He was walking around town carrying a kid's size knapsack on his back.

For some bizarre reason that image snapped me awake, and curtly tugged away my thumb from my mouth. The image that I had been drawn to had morphed into an awkward and geeky looking kid. And it bothered me bad.

I had to find a way to emancipate myself from his protective chains. Drawing back on memories from my rebellious adolescent years, I began to act recklessly and irresponsibly (like chewing with my mouth wide open and splattering jam on the floor). He called it off before I could dye my hair blue.

I had been attracted to the fatherly figure projected by Nathaniel all this while. As if he carried all my troubles away and implemented some order in my presumably chaotic life. It was the inner child in me that responded to him, not the woman in me. True, his protective nature provided me with a warm and fuzzy feeling but it turned quite stifling and suffocating in the end. Don't you go smacking my hands anymore you father imposter!

I eventually told myself I didn't want someone to daddy me around; one is enough, thank you very much. I think I'll do just fine tucking myself into bed from now on.

Reflections: It will always be your prerogative dear readers: Are you looking for a soul mate or a daddy-figure? It can be quite difficult to differentiate these two especially when you are in the thick of a budding relationship. I hear you. But the warning signs are usually there. It depends on whether you want to acknowledge their presence or not, that is.

Follow my advice: Let your inner child choose which fairy floss flavor you want to eat, and let the woman inside you pick the guys for your next date. Isn't life all about having a win-win situation and keeping everyone happy?

Contributor's info: Stella, 29, United Kingdom
Duration of courtship: 1 year
Ex category: Serial Cheater

Groovy music playing in the background, dimly lit dance floor wafting of perfume and eau de toilette and bodies swaying in a hedonistic trance. This was the setting that saw the first meeting of Jay and I.

We were both intoxicated with our surroundings and of course the few glasses of cocktails that we gulped down acted as the main culprit to our heady state of mind. It was just a matter of time our inhibitions went M.I.A (missing in action) and we started flirting barefacedly with one another.

Jay told me how he thought my charms and "alluring sexy body" were very attractive to him. I thought his macho body, dark athletic skin tone, height and good looks really stuck out from the crowd. Alright, he could be a big time player but he made my adrenalines running and pumping away. We continued our flirting game, whispered sweet nothings to each other's ears and danced the night away.

And then we left for our respective homes. That's right, nothing happened after that. Not yet at least.

A few weeks after that I went to my local library for some quiet time when I caught sight of a friend of mine at a table. He called out to me and said "Come over and let me introduce to you my handsome friend here". There was really no need for introductions as I was quite familiar with the guy. It was Jay.

We began talking and found out my mysterious dancing partner and I originated from the same city. Not only that, I even knew his younger sister from my high school. Coincidence? I think not. I took this as something of a powerful sign and we began to frequently go out with a bunch of other friends.

I enjoyed spending time with Jay and he was eager to bring me to the latest hot spots and interesting hangout places. I gathered that he was quite a man about town and an avid party-goer and found this aspect appealing. No harm in playing a bit with fire.

I would look forward to the end of each day when he would pick me up in his black sports car and drove around aimlessly. We would chat about our old hometown and he didn't hesitate from constantly complimenting me on my sexy body and wits. As any normal hot-blooded woman would, I soaked in all his compliments with delight. More, give me more!

After one night out at a pub, he brought me back to his bachelor pad for a visit. This would be the first time that we were alone together. I began admiring his collection on various sorts from classic music tapes, old telephones, radio sets, telescopes, old lamps to even raunchy pictures of models from bygone eras.

"This is surely a man with taste" I summed up before my eyes wandered off to the wastepaper basket next to his bed. I didn't mean to pry but I quickly saw evidence of some used condoms that appeared to have rendered its service just the previous night.

Ai yai yai......that should have been a blaring sign to me but it was much too late as I was already captivated and surrendered myself to his charms (and handsome looks). We officially became a couple that same night when I stayed over.

Not too long after that, I moved in. To our parents we were living in separate rooms but really mine was just a storage area. I happily assumed the duty as his cook, cleaner, entertainer, secretary plus other ad hoc roles. I was in utter bliss. I was in love with him and had fallen really hard for him. Even though at times I questioned about why I'm more on the giving end whereas he on the receiving end, I quickly pushed that thought aside and continued with my ironing. It didn't matter to me if I contributed more into the relationship.

Jay was quite a big spender and it took some effort in maintaining his car and artsy collections. I knew he only earned a meager amount from his delivery job but I soon learned he gave himself extra 'bonuses' now and then by obtaining it from the petty cash box – without his boss's knowledge.

The real tricky part of our relationship began when he moved to another state to start a new role. I stayed on as my career was moving up for me then. No matter how hard long-distance relationships would be I was very adamant we would overcome the odds.

Like any normal couple, we would argue occasionally over anything and everything. And since we were not living together anymore, I would conjure up stunts to test his loyalty towards me. During one of my trips to visit him, we got into a quarrel and I blurted out that I was returning home. I stormed out from the apartment and started running towards the train station. This was all on a pretense of course.

"No, you can't leave me!" Jay shouted before jumping on his bicycle to chase after me. The sight of a grown man on a little bicycle sent me laughing. I couldn't help it, it was hilarious! I quickly turned back to put a stop to this fiasco, funny but still a fiasco.

However as time went by I was beginning to suspect something was amiss when he began to act odd and was unavailable for most of the time I called him. The image of the used contraceptives found inside his dustbin flashed before me but I swiftly brushed it off.

This time it must be different in our case. We are now a couple, a happily attached couple. I'm sure he treasures and cherishes what we have now especially after all that I've done for him. After that little pep talk I hatched another plot to test him.

One weekend I secretly went to his apartment and called him from the lobby. I told him I was really going away for good this time. "No, you can't leave me!" Jay begged again and went on to convince me how much he loved me and how he couldn't live without me. I made myself sound very definite about it and then ended our conversation. I pictured him looking very lost and dejected and rushing out to catch the next train to my place.

Half and hour later no one came out. "Maybe he was too devastated to move," I thought. I called him again but this time told him the truth. "I was just pulling your leg! I am at your lobby so come down and pick me up you goose!" I was all prepared to make it up to him with a big bear hug.

But his reply this time caught me totally off guard. He said he couldn't come down to meet me. When I pressed for the reason, he finally admitted that he was actually at a friend's place. A lady friend's place to be precise. He even had the cheeks to go on and say he never meant to hurt me, that I deserved someone better and all that jazz.

I went hysterical. I was livid. I got the building's superintendent to open Jay's room door for me as he recognized me as his girlfriend. It was like a scene from a very bad nightmare. I saw no pictures of me in the apartment (he claimed he displayed them everywhere). His bed was freshly made up with the sheets neatly tucked into triangles at the corners (surely this act can only be done by a woman). I also detected strands of foreign long brown hair on his bed and when entering into his kitchen saw post-it notes on the fridge with messages of "Honey, please help me get some tomatoes" etc.

My heart immediately split into two halves. One for myself and the other for my parents. Since day one they had warned me to stay away from Jay. My folks saw through him and knew he was up to no good. I felt I had let them down.

I felt so mad at him I wanted to make him froth at his mouth. How long has he been cheating behind my back? Why couldn't I sense any of it? I thought he had tamed his wild ways and quit his roving eyes for me. He just said he loved me a few seconds ago!

Most of you won't disagree with me if I said Jay was one of the most reprehensible con artists there is. Nonetheless, I did partly blame myself for not heeding the signs that was scattered everywhere – literally. The first time that I had fell hard for someone; he turned out to be a serial cheater. He definitely perched at the lowest rung of the Pecking order.

It took me some time to recover, but I finally got over my heartache. As part of my newly proclaimed proactiveness, I now use him as an example of "Who Not to Date" whenever I'm privy to a male bantering session with my friends.

Good riddance to bad rubbish.

Reflections: I had allowed myself to be blinded by his appearance and sugar coated words. I even defied my ever wiser parents' advice to ditch that "poser". I followed my heart and put my brains at the back seat and ended with my heart broken into pieces.

I wanted so hard to make it work but it took a nasty revelation to wake me up from my slumber. I realized Jay was right – I did deserve someone better. At least not a serial cheater for sure.

They say first impressions are usually the truest. So when you discover used contraceptives at his place or ladies' undergarments strewn around, it's a good sign that he's still scouring the field and is not ready for a faithful girlfriend like you.

WHAT HAPPENS NOW?:
CYCLE OF GRIEVING AND
HEALING

Okay, so you have stopped obsessing about your breakup. No more "Why me?" and no more thoughts of signing up at the nearest nunnery. The mere mention of your ex's name has finally ceased to throw you into an uncontrollable frenzy, and you have discarded all plans to conjure up torturing ways to make him cry like a baby.

You know what? You deserve a great big pat on your back for arriving at this stage! It's about time missy!

Psychologists in general have conceded that when a person undergoes a loss in their life, the body's coping mechanism fires up causing the person to unwittingly journey through the cycle of grief.

I know this to be true as I did in fact went through all these stages, kicking and screaming in some phases and dissolving into a wet puddle in others.

97

Almost immediately after every breakup, I would hear myself uttering the same "Nah, we're not really over yet. Give us a few days and we'll be back together like two peas in a pod, gleefully licking our ice cream cones in the blistering heat." I dreadfully wanted to revert to our status quo. Did it matter how miserable he made me feel or how his obsessive compulsive behavior drove me up the wall? Of course not!

As for all his idiosyncrasies that once nearly drove me to my early grave, now I couldn't get enough of them. Oh how I would give up my favorite pair of Manolo's just to see him scratch and pick at his pimples-ridden back again. What I wouldn't do to make sure his boxers were folded into neat triangles. It was quite apparent that I was undergoing some withdrawal symptoms.

I was convinced beyond any reasonable doubt that I couldn't live without him, and losing him would mean losing the one guy I was destined to marry and bear children with.

I would proceed to fantasize about how my ex would deliver an obscene number of multi-colored roses to my office, pleading for us to be reunited. Or me being greeted by a humongous size of a teddy bear spilling out from my bed with a huge 'I'm sorry' card tucked under its armpit. Other members of the household can also forget about using the house phone as he will definitely call any second now to reconcile.

When concerned friends asked about the separation or offered advice during this trying time of mine, I would shoot them with an irritated look before barking out "Who said we were separated? We are just having a time off that's all! Now go back to powdering your noses in the loo."

This is what they call the **denial** phase. You can say my mind was somewhat deluded. It's akin to the It Ain't Over Til the Fat Lady Sings syndrome, and as long as she ain't singing, I'll be clinging on to the relationship like a leech to a meaty back side.

And then, almost as quickly as denial overcame me, I found myself engulfed by fury and unexplainable rage. Ladies, welcome to the world of **anger**. It is eerily comparable to the phrase 'Hell hath no fury like a woman scorned'. I pictured myself holding a pitchfork with two little horns sprouting out from my head.

I was mad at the universe, mad at the bunch of bananas and mad at the drooling baby. It didn't matter who and what it was, I was just seething with a lot of angst. But my biggest ferocity was unmistakably directed towards my ex. That wretched neantherdal, I wish he would crawl back into his cave and get mauled by a saber tooth tiger.

I mean, how dare he abandon me and left me to fend for myself? He suddenly became my sworn enemy, my arch rival. His cute curly locks and swooning voice assaulted my sight and hearing just by the thought of it. I would air gag by the mention of anything remotely connected to him. There were instances when I found myself calling him up during the calm of the night and bellowing out unspeakable profanities at him, and only stopping to slam down the phone upon the passing of my moment of temporary insanity.

I was hurting and reeling from the pain still, and I wanted to make sure he was hurting just as much, if not more. If he cherished our relationship as much as I did, his duration of suffering would be indicative of how much he treasured our past love i.e. the longer the better. And should he commit the unthinkable sin of recovering faster than I did, man, things can get pretty ugly then.

You can say I was saved from becoming a potential quack job when I watched a rerun of Fatal Attraction one night and saw disturbing similarities between myself and Glenn Close. I decided I didn't want to wait until I whipped up a pot of rabbit stew to finally come to my senses. Spare the fluffy animals I say!

I must admit, I was never a savvy bargainer. During one account of my haggling attempts at a flea market, the seller made an initial offer of a mere $1 discount. I grabbed the merchandise, paid the amount and sprinted away so fast the seller didn't even have time to turn around to mutter contempt at my expected retort. Nonetheless, I soon discovered my hidden **bargaining** talent when my emotions soon moved on to one that tried to desperately salvage whatever that was left.

We can still be best friends right? I don't really see it as an issue if I were to continue joining your family dinners and having sleepovers after that. What about allocating Mondays, Wednesdays, Fridays and Sundays for us as a weekly catch up? You know that couples only getaway during Christmas? I'm sure it's just semantics......want to go?

Imagine you just dropped a basket full of eggs on the floor. Do you frantically pick up the broken shells thinking it can all be mended back together? No, as it will just be a futile attempt wouldn't it? We both know very well that the bits and pieces can never be returned to its original state. Such is the case with broken relationships as well.

The bargainer in me was urging me at this point to cut my losses. I had invested time, money and the best years of my lives in some cases in my relationships. This gave me every right to get something out of it, didn't it? Truth of the matter was, emotionally I had suffered the biggest loss. I thought I could compensate and fill the void by making him run some menial errands for me, pretending to fall sick so that he can care for me, etc. Anything to create a false sense of exclusivity. I just wasn't ready to cut the umbilical cord as doing it would mean severing all ties with him and cementing the hard fact that we were no longer a couple, but two unattached individuals.

Depression. A feeling of desolation crept upon me and hurled me into another realm of emotion. This time round I was trapped inside a deep dark hole. No matter how hard I struggled to climb out, I kept slipping back into the bleak abyss. My mind was the abyss and stuck I was to the image of my ex and fleeting images of our happy moments. Everywhere I went and everywhere I looked, people morphed into my ex….even inanimate objects morphed into him. Gee, do I know that lamp post?

At this stage, I no longer lingered on any hope to reconcile, to bargain or to make him weep like a girl. My midnight bouts of a rather violent case of 'verbal diarrhea' have also stopped. I succeeded in prying myself away from his family get togethers and quit propositioning to him the idea of becoming a non-couple 'couple'.

After an emotional roller coaster ride, I finally allowed reality to set in. The bitter truth was that we have parted ways. And no, he won't come a galloping to plant a wet one on me and waking me up from this seemingly horrid dream.

There were a lot of moping at this stage and my inability to focus on almost everything. I was literally bummed out. You could have fed me a plate of worms and I would have thought it was funny-tasting spaghetti. In hindsight, I now see that I was in fact mourning. At times, I would wake up feeling totally rejuvenated and shock the curlers out of my nanny by doing 50 lapses in the pool. But after lunch you'd see me half dragging myself across the hall, shaking my head and mumbling something to myself.

Just when I was about to resign to a lifetime of solitude, with the neighborhood kids calling me the 'crazy cat lady', I sensed myself being lifted and embraced by an aura of peace and tranquility. It's like that feeling when you are recovering from a bout of flu and your ears and nose miraculously become unblocked. Hey, the birds are chirping and I can smell that foul stench from the drains again. Hooray!

Last stop: **acceptance**. Acceptance of the demise of a relationship that was never meant to be. This is the homerun, where I learnt to cherish all the good times I shared with my partner then, and the invaluable lessons I can take away from all the less desirable experiences.

My ex had been successfully exorcised from my mind and body. I have been set free! As if a burnt out light bulb had ignited itself in my head, I could finally see clearly now. I recognized that as long as I was clutching to the old and dead, the new will never come into my life. It was high time I made space in my heart and mind, and chuck away the pajamas that I had been wearing for 6 months.

So what if this was another unsuccessful relationship? Like the saying goes, it's better to have loved and lost than not to have loved at all right? And sure, some of you may find yourself thinking you've hit the final acceptance base only to be flung across to the first denial stage again. No one said this cycle was a one way, straightforward passage.

Exactly like a roller coaster ride, you won't know where you'll be going next, which turn or curve will hit you. But I do know, speaking from experience, that it is a necessary evil, I mean spiral we need to go through in order for us to grow. And just like a roller coaster ride, after each whirlwind trip we'll come out fully invigorated, recharged and eagerly wanting for the next one (albeit a little woozy in the stomach).

Top 10 things you can do post-breakup

- Do stuff that you've always been good at and makes you happy. Paint, cook, making paper dolls etc. You and only YOU can make yourself the happiest!
- Take this time to rediscover and reinvent yourself. List down the top three vocations that you've always wanted to pursue. You'll never know, perhaps there's a singer/comedian in you.
- Have a girls' night out, or a pajama party. Nothing feels more liberating than letting your hair down, gorging on sinful cakes and spending the whole night yacking about, what else…..men!
- Spend some quality time alone - have a 'me' day. Go on a meditation retreat in the hills, rejuvenate with a full body massage or pay a visit to your favorite pedicure and manicure shop and ask for the works. After all, borrowing the words from a famous ad, "I'm worth it".
- Immerse in a week-long sweat-inducing and adrenalin-pumping exercise regimen. Reward yourself by having a nice cuppa with the cute gym instructor afterwards.
- Retail therapy. Need I say more?
- Invite a bunch of good friends and hit the town for some serious grooving and booty shaking. In any case, there's bound to be some eye candy at the latest dance club.
- Try sharing your story with a qualified counselor, psychiatrists, family members or a trustworthy confidant. They might just utter one sentence that can change your whole perspective in relationship and love forever.

- Take a piece of paper and list twenty things you like about yourself. Now next to it, simply write the word "Can be over-emotional during certain times of the month". See, your virtues beat your shortcomings by a landslide!
- Last but not least, you can always start writing a satirical memoir on all your botched relationships. I hear it can be quite therapeutic.

Top 10 things you can do post a really ugly breakup

(WARNING: Do not try this unsupervised!)

- Bake gingerbread man cookies with all your exes' faces. Then devour them one by one. Slowly.
- Tell your ex you think football is a stupid game and his favorite team sucks.
- In front of him, flirt shamelessly with three-haired Moe the bartender. Go on, let him know what he's missing.
- Tell your ex the whole world notices about his receding hairline and his sagging man boobs.
- Try some aversion therapy. Stare at his picture for a few seconds and then get your friend to smack you in the face. Not too hard of course and don't mess up the hair!
- Gather all his belongings left in your home, and have a small BBQ in your backyard. Starters – Shish keBOB; Main – Chicken ala KEITH; Sides – JACKet potatoes and salad.
- Call up his mom and dad, and tell them your ex was the real culprit that broke their family heirloom. I'm sure the wrongly accused family cat will be eternally grateful to you.
- Send a big bouquet of flowers to your ex at his office. Attach an even bigger card to it, signing it off with 'From your sweetie pie Maxwell." I'm sure it'll raise quite a few *queer* eyebrows.

- Cut out a picture of him, blow it up to A3 size and invite the neighborhood kids to come play 'Pin the tail on the man's arse'.
- Invite him for a post-breakup dinner, and accidentally drop a few pine nuts in his pasta when he isn't looking. Apologize profusely for the 'accident' – how can you remember he was allergic to them?! Assure him his coin-size warts will disappear fairly quickly.

Last Few Words (Inspirational affirmations)

1. It's not you, it's him.
2. It's his loss, not yours.
3. Don't get even, get curvaceous and successful.
4. One woman's crème Brule is another woman's poison.
5. Take everything and everyone else seriously except yourself.
6. Don't shortchange yourself. Why settle for Mr. Mediocre when you can have Mr. Wonderful.
7. The only time a woman can change a man is when he's still in diapers.
8. Love thy neighbor (even if she stole your ex).
9. There are plenty of fishes in the sea. If anything there is always the crustacean.
10. To err is human, to forgive is divine. You know you are capable of divinity.
11. Men - can't live with them, can't live without them. At least you can train them to put the toilet seat back down.
12. Once bitten, twice shy. If there's a third then you should ask yourself why.
13. When the going gets tough, the tough sometimes go for a facial and foot massage.
14. To binge or not to binge, you really shouldn't even be considering that question.

15. It takes more muscles to frown than to smile. The latter sounds less of a hassle.
16. If he's not ready to commit, he's really telling you the truth. Thank him for his honesty.
17. You don't need anything or anyone to make you happy. You only need you (a good manicure never hurt).
18. When one door closes, another one spreads wide open.
19. You need to taste the bitter to appreciate the sweet.
20. Dating is part of a grand elimination process; it's moving you closer to your end target.
21. A relationship that starts with betrayal ends in betrayal. You should drop him like a nut.
22. Once a cheater is almost always a cheater. You should drop him like a bigger nut.
23. He broke your heart; don't let him break your spirit too.
24. If he seemed too good to be true, he probably was.
25. Anger begets anger….it'll just be one vicious cycle then wouldn't it?
26. You're 30 and desperately single? Embrace it! Washing his boxers and changing nappies can wait a few more years.
27. There are three things you can do to meet that "Ideal" man of yours. Network, network and network.
28. Never say never.
29. A breakup is a blessing in disguise. Remember all the clouds and their silver linings?
30. What you want may not be what you need. I wanted George Clooney but ended up with his total opposite. He was nothing I wanted, but everything I ever dreamed of having.
31. Where have all the good men gone? They are somewhere. Have faith and he'll manifest at the opportune time.
32. Men are like parking spots - All the good ones are taken and the ones left are either too short or handicapped. Just kidding. There's always the next level.

33. Be the bigger person. Say "Hi" to him the next time you bump into each other instead of running off.
34. Happiness is a journey; the destination is when the ride comes to a stop.
35. The old and kaput needs to be chucked away to make room for the spanking new.
36. Things happen for a reason. Our Creator doesn't make mistakes.
37. Men are like a box of chocolates. You'll never know which one has nuts.
38. It's better to be single and happy than attached and miserable.
39. Dated one too many nutcases? Great! You can start writing your own book.
40. You are as young as your heart feels. Don't let age pester you into settling for second best.
41. Learn from the mistakes of others.
42. Laughter is truly the best medicine. Laugh with yourself, be your own biggest fan.
43. Love is a many splendid thing. No one said it was an easy thing though.
44. He still loves me, he loves me not. He still loves me, he loves me not. If he hasn't called it's probably not.
45. Love is not having to say you're sorry. Unless it was the guy's fault.
46. This too shall pass.
47. They say love is blind. That must be absolutely true especially for those close encounters with the freakish kind.
48. If you are the dumper, execute it with style. If you are the dumpee, handle it like the gracious lady that you are. You can bitch about your ex beau afterwards.
49. You are a survivor. Lest us forget women and their higher threshold for pain.
50. Have no regrets. You gave it your all.